GW09866438

Pony Racer

Pony Racer

LUCY JOHNSON

Forelock Books

Published by Forelock Books Ltd.

49 Barfields, Bletchingley, Surrey RH1 4RA

www.forelock-books.co.uk

First published in 2015

Typeset by LKS Designs

Printed in the EU on behalf of Latitude Press Ltd.

A CIP catalogue record for this book is available from the British Library

ISBN 978-0-9928-7088-1

For Toby

Chapter 1

'Everything is rubbish,' thought Tom as he hugged his knees into his chest. He tried hard to fight back the tears but one by one they tumbled down his cheeks like raindrops dripping down a windowpane. A gentle breeze ruffled the grass around him and the trees whispered as they swayed. Tom was small and skinny for his age with dark brown hair and huge brown eyes. He'd been with the Heavens for two weeks now and he really liked living at Hilltop House. But he was in trouble again so he had fled to the fields in front of the house to escape.

He hadn't meant to steal. It's just that he had felt hungry. And he hated feeling hungry. It reminded him of his mother and the terrible things she did to him, so he'd gone to the larder to steal some biscuits. And Mrs Heaven had caught him. He'd run from the kitchen. Mrs Heaven had called something after him, but he hadn't heard what it was. Now he sat on the hill-side overlooking the woodland below and the cliffs that dropped down to the beach in the distance.

Everything had been going so well. He'd met Jim and Mandy Heaven and their two children many times in the foster home before he had come to live with them. Emily was nine, the same age as him, and Ted was eleven. Although he never said much, he liked them. He thought they liked him too. Mr and Mrs Heaven had even said he could call them Jim and Mandy, but he preferred not to. 'Now I've ruined everything,' he thought to himself. He'd been caught stealing and now they knew he was bad, just like his mother always told him, and he'd be sent back to the foster home. He wanted to return to the house, and say sorry, and that he didn't mean to take the biscuits. But he couldn't. They wouldn't understand and he didn't know how to tell them he was scared he'd be locked up again. He didn't want to talk about that, and boys weren't supposed to get scared anyway.

He watched the two ponies standing under the big tree half way down the hill. He knew their names were Skip and Henry. He stared at them for a while, distracted, wondering where the third pony, Leo, was. Then he remembered his troubles. Screwing his eyes shut, he placed his hands against his ears so he could block out the sounds of the countryside. He sat like that for what seemed like an age, until he felt a soft blowing against his cheek. Shuddering he turned his back against it. But the strange blowing continued. Tom opened his eyes and, glancing up, he jumped as he saw Leo peering at him, blowing gently down his nostrils.

Leo was the smallest of the three ponies, and a dark bay colour with a white blaze down the centre of his face and four white socks. Tom had barely uttered any words since he'd been at Hilltop House, but he'd taken in everything, including the names of all the animals. He had often watched the ponies, but he had never gone near them, even though Mr and Mrs Heaven and the children had encouraged him to get to know them.

There were two horses too. They were called Elvis and Chilli and they were enjoying a summer holiday in Hilltop House's best meadow in the valley below. They were racehorses and ran in point-to-points during the winter and spring – although Tom had no idea what that meant. He just knew they were very big and very special to the Heavens.

"Why are you blowing on me? Go away Leo," cried Tom, and turned his back on the pony.

Leo gently nudged him.

"I said GO AWAY," Tom shouted pulling his hood over his head.

Leo nudged him again, and then nuzzled him softly along his back.

"Stop it Leo," said Tom ignoring him until Leo gave him an almighty shove. Tom rolled sideways and ended up on his back. He lay there staring right into the dark brown eyes of the pretty pony. Leo stood quietly, his head down low, not quite touching Tom.

"Why won't you just leave me alone?" said Tom. He started crying again, suddenly feeling terribly alone in a scary horrible world.

Leo stood quite still, his ears pricked as he listened to the sobs coming from the sad little boy whose blue hoodie was far too big for him and who had stick-thin legs poking from long, grey shorts. He gave the boy another small nudge. Tom tried to make himself invisible, pulling his hoodie around him but Leo didn't give up.

Tom felt confused. Why did the pony stay? Tom had always been told to go away and he knew it was best to obey. When he wasn't being told to disappear, he was just ignored. Most of the time it was if he didn't exist. Until he reached his eighth birthday. That's when his mum started locking him in the cupboard. He'd sit in silence in his squalid home, trying not to bring attention to himself so that his mum would forget he was there. But every night she locked him up, leaving him there for hours on end, sometimes days, chucking in a packet of cheap sausage rolls and a bottle of water. Unless it was a school day. Then she never forgot him, and every morning she marched him to the school gates bang on time.

"You are not going to go away, are you?" Tom reached out his hand. Leo sniffed it and then gave it a lick.

"That feels funny," said Tom. He nearly giggled as he snatched his hand back and then gently offered it again. Leo rested his soft muzzle on it. Sitting up, Tom gently scratched the pony down the middle of his face. Leo stood quietly by his side, nuzzling him every now and again.

Eventually Tom stood up. Leo was 13.2hh and his wither was level with Tom's nose, so he could see over the top to the other side. Tom tentatively ran his hands along Leo's neck and across his back. Leo stood patiently.

"You like this don't you?" Tom said, feeling the pony's soft warm hair through the palm of his hand. He didn't feel scared at all, even though he'd never touched a pony before. Slowly his face started to light up as he allowed himself a hint of a smile. It seemed like a long time since he had smiled properly. But all of a sudden he flopped into the grass and started sobbing again. Leo jumped back and trotted away, startled. Tom felt so alone in the huge field: "There's no point being friends Leo. As soon as they find me they'll send me away," he cried.

Very slowly Leo edged his way back over to Tom and nudged him again.

"Why have you come back?" Tom sobbed, turning away from the pony.

Leo pushed him again. Tom couldn't resist. He stood up and put his arms around the pony's neck and then put his cheek against the warm neck and closed his eyes. "Everyone hates me except you," he said quietly.

After a minute or two, Tom unwrapped himself and, feeling a glimmer of happiness, skipped across the field. Leo followed. Tom ran. Leo trotted behind him. Dodging one way then another, they ran through the field. Forgetting his troubles, Tom laughed as he leapt and ran, Leo always just a few strides behind as he bucked and cantered along. Eventually, Tom collapsed into the grass, and Leo stopped by him.

"You're the best," said Tom reaching up to hug him again. "Will you be my best friend? I've never had a best friend." Leo turned and set off at a sharp canter. "Hey wait for me. I thought you were my friend," shouted Tom.

Leo stopped and Tom caught up. Then he set off again, bucking and squealing while Tom chased him. The air filled with laughter and for the first time in a very long time Tom felt happy.

Chapter 2

"He'll be alright that one," said Mr Heaven quietly to his wife Mandy as they watched Tom from the garden, which was next to the pony field.

"I think he will, but we've a long way to go yet. He's been through such a lot for such a small lad," said Mrs Heaven. "It's just such a shame he ran off in a panic before I could explain he didn't need to worry about the biscuits."

"Let's keep him busy with the animals. If he begins to trust them, it'll be a start," Mr Heaven replied.

It was the weekend and Mr Heaven had a day off from his busy veterinary practice in the nearby village of Todbury. Mr and Mrs Heaven and Emily and Ted lived in a big, rambling house with a huge garden and several fields on a hill above the South Devon coastline.

"It's good to see him smiling. I'll bet anything it's a long time since he's done that," said Mrs Heaven who was a part-time teacher in the local primary school.

Emily appeared through the French doors that led from the kitchen. Her long blonde hair was tied up in a ponytail, and she wore purple jodphurs, a pink T-shirt and brown leather ankle boots. Close behind followed Ted who had a mop of brown curly hair and wore jeans and a red sweatshirt.

"Mum, are we going for a ride now?" asked Emily slipping her arm around her mother's waist.

Mrs Heaven kissed her on the top of her head. "In a while

Emily. We're just watching Tom for a minute. He's getting on very well with Leo."

"What's he doing out there?" asked Emily.

"He thought he was going to be in trouble when I saw him in the kitchen taking some food, and before I had time to say anything, he ran out into the ponies' field."

"And you, young lady, must be extra nice to him," said Mr Heaven rubbing his daughter's hair fondly.

"It's difficult being nice to someone who never, ever says anything," said Emily.

"All he does is sit there and do nothing," added Ted.

Their parents nodded. Then they heard a shriek of laughter and saw Leo go bucking off down the field before cantering back to Tom and skidding to halt in front of him. They watched as Tom reached forward and scratched the pony's head again. Leo seemed to put his head under the boy's arm and the pair stood side by side, gazing down to the sea.

"I've never seen Leo do that before. Why doesn't he do that with me?" asked Emily.

"For some reason that pair have bonded, and it could be just what Tom needs after everything he has been through," said Mrs Heaven.

Mr Heaven agreed: "The kid needs a break and I have a feeling Hilltop House might just be the sort of place he needs."

"Anyway, come on Mum. Aren't we going for a ride now?" interrupted Emily.

Her mum nodded: "I'll just finish pegging this washing up. You two grab the headcollars and go and fetch Skip and Henry. They've been watching Leo from under the tree."

"What about Leo? Won't he want to come in too?" Ted said as he walked towards the garden gate, which in turn led to the stable block.

"Take his headcollar too. Tom might want to lead him in," said Mrs Heaven picking up her basket of washing.

The stables were in an L-shape at the far side of the house. Each stable door had a nameplate for the three ponies and the race-horses Elvis and Chilli. Beside the stables was an open barn, which contained all the hay and straw, and next to that was the tack-room. Behind the stables was a large arena filled with show jumps of all colours and sizes, and two lines of traffic cones spaced about six feet apart.

Ted grabbed Henry's navy blue headcollar and lead rope and a red one for Leo. Emily took the pink one for Skip. They opened the metal gate quietly and slipped through. Suddenly a sharp breeze pulled it out of Ted's hand and swung it shut with a huge clang. Henry and Skip, who had been dozing peacefully in the sunshine, looked up startled. They both snorted and went galloping off away from the children. Leo, sensing there was fun to be had, joined them, and the three went cantering around the field.

"We'll never catch them now," wailed Emily and flung her headcollar into the grass and started crying.

"Stop being such a big baby," retorted Ted and went running off after them.

The ponies galloped even more.

"Don't just stand there," yelled Ted to Tom. "Help us catch them."

"Chasing them won't help. You are just frightening them," said Tom.

"We do know that, but we need to catch them. What's your suggestion, clever clogs?" Ted ran past and nearly tripped in the long grass. "And what do you know about ponies anyway?" he shouted.

"Nothing I guess, but I don't think chasing them will do any good," Tom replied. It was the most he had said during the entire time he had been at Hilltop House.

Ted stopped running and as soon as he did the ponies stopped too. Emily ran over to the boys, the tears streaked down her face, sniffling.

"Stop crying Emily. It's not the end of the world. Look they've stopped running now."

"If we walk away from them up to the hedge, they might come to find out what we are doing," said Tom.

"I suppose we could try it," Ted nodded noticing how much the ponies had already calmed down.

The three children set off together walking very slowly away from the ponies. Leo was the first to trot after them. Soon Skip and Henry followed. The children stopped walking and stood quite still. Leo nudged Tom.

"Put this on him," said Ted passing him the red headcollar.

Tom took it, inspected it and then placed it on the top of Leo's head so that his ears poked through. Then he wrapped the rope around the pony's neck. Ted and Emily started giggling.

"What are you laughing at?" Tom looked bemused.

"Pull the rope and see what happens," Emily said.

Tom pulled it and the headcollar fell on the ground. Tom picked it up again and tried to work out how the contraption worked.

"Here, let us help," said Ted and they showed Tom what to do.

"Just hold the rope now, so that he doesn't go off for another canter. Stand by his side, rather than in front, when you go to lead him off."

Ted put the blue headcollar on Henry, who by this time was standing patiently in line, while Emily caught Skip.

"Come on you naughty ponies. Time for a carrot and then we are going to do practise some gymkhana races." Emily skipped ahead, followed by Ted and Henry.

Tom and Leo stood side by side. "Come on then Leo. Time to go." Tom stood directly in front of him, put both hands at the top of the rope near the clip and pulled. Leo pulled against him. Tom pulled some more. Leo put his ears flat back and refused to move.

"Hey, hey," shouted Tom to Emily and Ted. "Leo won't move."

But the others had already disappeared into the yard. As he yelled, Tom released his grip slightly. Leo moved half a step forward.

"Oh so you are coming now are you?" said Tom, facing him and pulling as hard as he could.

Leo dug his toes in again.

"I thought you were my friend," cried Tom, letting go of the rope and sinking to the ground sobbing uncontrollably.

With the tension released from the rope, Leo stepped over to Tom and gave him a nudge.

"Just leave me alone Leo."

But Leo stood patiently until eventually Tom stood up and, grabbing the rope, he walked to the stables with Leo by his side.

"You just didn't like being dragged did you?" asked Tom rubbing the pony's neck as they walked.

"Well done Tom," said Mrs Heaven who had watched everything. "You worked that out pretty quickly. Pop him in his stable over there," she said, following him.

"I'll show you how to take it off." She undid the buckle and slipped the headcollar off Leo's head.

"Here you go Tom. Put it in the tackroom. And Tom, we do understand... everything. This is your home now. Don't worry about the biscuits."

She saw a glimmer of a smile and went to give him a hug, but he quickly turned, muttering, "Yes Mrs Heaven."

"Mandy, Tom, call me Mandy," she laughed.

"Yes Mrs Heaven," he called back.

Emily tacked up Skip and led him out to the arena. "Can I jump on now, Mum?" she asked.

"Yes, then walk him around to warm him up. We'll practise cones today. Are you ready Ted?"

"Coming Mum," shouted Ted leading Henry.

"How about you Tom? Would you like to watch?"

"No," replied Tom.

Mrs Heaven didn't push him. "We'll see you in a bit then," she said.

Soon the children were trotting and cantering around the school and weaving in and out of the cones. Laugher rang out as they practised their gymkhana games.

Emily trotted over to her mum. "Where's Tom?"

"He's doing just fine with Leo. He'll come up if he wants to. If you look, you can see him in the stable."

"Do you think he'll ever be happy again, Mum? He was brilliant in the field. He seemed to know what to do when the ponies were galloping around."

"I think he'll be just fine. And I think the ponies may be the key to helping him feel wanted and loved."

From the stable, Tom could see the children having fun in the arena. "One day I am going to race on ponies," he promised Leo who cocked an ear back, listening. "I don't know how 'cos I don't know how to ride like they do. But I will, one day. Me and you, Leo, galloping along."

Tom could hear the children whooping and yelling with Mrs Heaven shouting instructions and the ponies cantering all over the place. Peering out of the stable door he thought it all looked completely bonkers but great fun.

"Yep, you and me Leo. We'll be doing that soon," he promised.

Soon the children clattered back into the yard on their ponies.

"Take their tack off and hose them down. They are very sweaty," said Mrs Heaven.

"I beat Ted. I beat Ted," sang Emily annoyingly.

Ted picked up a sopping wet sponge and flung it at her, getting her square in the face.

"I hate you Ted," said Emily grabbing a bucket of water and tipping it over his head.

Ted picked up the hosepipe and sprayed her, chasing her as she tried to escape.

Turning off the tap, Mrs Heaven shouted: "Home now! Both of you. I have told you before you are not to have water fights in the stable yard. You will frighten the ponies."

Emily and Ted skulked off back to the garden, annoyed that they had been told off, although secretly Ted was relieved. He loved riding ponies. He hated doing any of the work such as mucking out and grooming.

"I thought it looked like fun," said Tom creeping out of Leo's stable.

Mrs Heaven was surprised to hear him speak. "Yes Tom, it is a lot of fun, but better to do it in the garden. Horses and ponies can get startled very easily and that's when accidents happen."

"Why?" asked Tom.

"When ponies are frightened or unsure of something, their natural reaction is to run away. That's why they are often called flight animals."

"Is that why they ran away when Ted and Emily went running after them in the field?"

"That's exactly right, Tom," said Mrs Heaven as they walked back to the house together. "Tom, you don't need to worry about leaving here. This is your home now," she continued gently.

"When are you going to punish me about the biscuits?" he asked.

"Tom, listen to me. You are not going to be punished."

"But you will do soon, won't you? You're saying everything is fine now but soon you'll punish me. 'Cos that's what happens. I'll think everything is OK and then bam, you'll bash me or lock me up or something." He trembled as memories of the dark cupboard came flooding back, shouting to be let out, and banging on the door, but no-one ever heard him.

"Tom, you need to trust us. Nothing bad is going to happen here."

"But Mum always told me I am bad. That's why she locked me up. And I stole biscuits. But I don't want to be hungry again."

"Tom, you are not bad. If you were, Leo wouldn't have come anywhere near you."

"I think he likes me," said Tom very quietly.

"He certainly does. He's taken to you straight away, and if you were bad, he wouldn't want to know."

Tom said nothing, but her words made him feel warm inside. He couldn't explain why, but he felt happier. He looked up at her. His expression didn't change. But Mrs Heaven knew at that moment that Tom would be OK. She held out her hand and Tom went to grab it, before deciding against it. It was a very positive start though thought Mrs Heaven.

Later on the children all sat down to eat their supper together.

"Leo loves Tom, Leo loves Tom," said Emily, trying to annoy the boys at the table. Little did she realise that by trying to be annoying, she was saying just what Tom needed to hear. He wolfed down his food, and then picked up his plate and licked it. Emily was about to yell out "Eugh," but her mum caught her eye just in time and mouthed the word "No" to stop her from embarrassing him.

"Would you like me to teach you how to play Minecraft?" asked Ted.

"No." He went to sit on the windowsill and stared outside like he had every evening since he'd arrived at Hilltop House.

Mrs Heaven watched him, wondering what he was thinking about.

"He'll be fine. Keep him busy with the ponies and they'll teach him plenty," said Mr Heaven, putting his arm around his wife's shoulders.

"I hope so. He deserves to be happy."

Mrs Heaven gave them hugs at bedtime, except Tom, who shied away, and one by one they went to their rooms.

Tom's room was paradise to him. The curtains and duvet matched. There was a soft rug on the floor, a huge beanbag to sink into and shelves laden with books and toys.

He quickly changed and dived under his bed covers. On his pillow was a fluffy pony, all soft and floppy. He looked at it and wondered who had put it there. Not really caring, he cuddled it to his chest. He'd never had a soft toy before.

Outside his bedroom door a soft light lit the landing. He could just make out the sound of Mr and Mrs Heaven chatting downstairs. He soon fell asleep but woke up feeling a sudden rush of fear. He couldn't explain it but he knew he had to get out of the house to safety, to Leo.

Chapter 3

"Tom, Miss George, your social worker, is coming to see you this morning," called Mrs Heaven.

"I'll wake him," Mr Heaven bounded up the stairs. "Come on Tom, time to get up," he said opening the door.

Tom's bed was empty. Mr Heaven checked the bathroom. He wasn't there. "Tom?" he called.

Mrs Heaven came rushing to the bottom of the stairs. "What is it Jim? Where's Tom?"

"He's gone."

"He can't have gone. He seemed OK yesterday." Frantically, Mrs Heaven rushed out of the kitchen door.

"Tom!" she called loudly as Jim joined her. "Jim, please call Miss George and let her know." She shouted again. "Tom, please come back."

She went to the spot in the field where Tom had been sitting the day before. He wasn't there. She rushed past the stables and started to run up the drive. Two pony heads looked over their doors inquisitively, wondering what all the commotion was about. Mrs Heaven hesitated, was about to run on, and then stopped.

'Something's not right. Why isn't Leo looking over his door?' she thought, rushing over. She peered over the door and didn't know whether to laugh or cry at what she saw. Leo was lying flat out in the deep straw. Tom was fast asleep with his head resting on Leo's outstretched neck. The pony gave a low whicker to Mrs Heaven but he didn't move as she crept in and knelt in the straw beside Tom. Very gently, she placed a hand on his shoulder and gave him the smallest of nudges. Tom slowly stirred while she spoke in a low, soft voice, not wanting to startle him.

"It's OK Tom. It's just me, Mandy."

"Wh-wh-where am I?" he asked. "Oh Leo," he remembered and hugged him.

"Let's let Leo get up now Tom. He hasn't moved a muscle as he didn't want to wake you."

Tom stood up, and Leo did the same.

"What are you doing here love?"

"I thought it was all a dream and I was going to be taken away. I feel safe here, with Leo."

Mrs Heaven reached out to him and Tom allowed her to hug him.

"You are safe with us too. I promise you that."

"And you won't lock me up if I'm bad? I mean I never meant to be bad it's just that I was always hungry and the hunger was so bad I stole food."

"That won't happen to you ever again. I promised you that yesterday and it's the same today. But you have to trust me, like you trust Leo."

At that moment, Mr Heaven, Emily and Ted peered over the door.

"Hello Tom. Your own bed not good enough for you?" joked Jim Heaven. "Time for breakfast, then Miss George will be here to see how you are getting on."

They all walked back together to Hilltop House.

Emily swung from her father's hand, Ted walked with his mother, and Tom hung back a few steps behind on his own.

"Come on Tom," called Mr Heaven.

"I'm fine here," he replied.

"You're part of our family now, and that means we always wait for each other," laughed Mr Heaven.

Tom let himself smile. Maybe everything is going to be OK he thought. Then, feeling brave, he asked: "Could I have a go at riding Leo today?"

"That's a brilliant idea. Lets do that after Miss George has been," said Mrs Heaven.

Tom gave them a glimmer of a smile before setting off running towards the house. Ted and Emily followed.

"Wait for us Tom," they shouted and the three ran off together.

"Something has unlocked in that little boy, and I have a feeling it's all down to Leo," said Mrs Heaven.

"The pony certainly adores him, and that's helping Tom feel wanted, but I think it will be a long time before he trusts humans again," replied Mr Heaven.

Chapter 4

"So Tom, before you can ride, you need to brush your pony and pick out his feet."

"Why? He'll only go and get muddy again."

"You need to brush off the mud so that his tack doesn't rub. It's also really good for his muscles. And you need to pick out his feet to make sure there are no stones in them."

"Seems like a lot of work to me, just to sit on a pony," muttered Tom.

"Riding ponies does require a lot of hard work, including mucking out stables."

"So you do all this work everyday, just to be able to ride?"

"In a nutshell, yes," said Mrs Heaven. "But for now we'll just concentrate on the good bits. This is the saddle and this is the bridle. One goes on the head, and the other on the back." She quickly tacked up Leo. "OK, let's get you up."

She led Leo to the mounting block and explained to Tom how to get on.

"Yep," he said only half listening and leaping into the saddle instead of following her instructions. But he was so light and nimble he swung himself easily over Leo's back and sat down gently. "S'good up here." He looked around enjoying the view. "Come on then, let's go."

"Not so fast Tom. Here's how you hold the reins...and this is where your foot goes – it's called the stirrup."

"Yep, got all that. Let's go."

Mrs Heaven had seen a fair few children ride, but never had she encountered a child who seemed so at home on the back of a pony. He didn't clamp on. He wasn't rigid. He just relaxed his body into the movement of the pony.

"How are you feeling?"

"Brilliant, Mrs Heaven. Feels like I was born to be up here."

"Mandy!"

"Brilliant Mandy."

He leant forward and patted Leo on the neck. "You're a good pony Leo," he murmured. Leo flicked an ear back as if he was listening.

"Let's walk a few times around the school." Mrs Heaven led Leo while Tom concentrated on his reins.

"So if I pull, he stops and if I let them go slack he goes again?"

"Not quite Tom, but nearly. You feel with the reins and you ask with the leg. They are called aids and they are what we use to control horses and ponies."

"I get it," Tom said and gave Leo a trial kick.

Leo leapt forward startled at the indignity of being kicked.

Unperturbed, Tom quietly said: "Woah Leo." Leo stopped. "Sorry," he patted the pony. "I never liked being kicked either. I promise I won't do that again."

Mandy was quite amazed at how at home Tom was in the saddle. "Let's try some trotting. You rise up and down to the rhythm of the trot. Up down, up down, one two, one two." She jogged beside him keeping a hand on the reins. For a stride or two Tom jolted about in the saddle before picking up the rhythm. "This is dead easy!" He trotted around the school like a child who had had many riding lessons.

Mrs Heaven was impressed with his progress but soon said: "That's enough for one day."

"But it's so easy. Can't we carry on?"

"We could but your own muscles aren't used to riding and you'll be stiff tomorrow. Small steps at a time."

"Okedoke Mrs Heaven," he said jumping down from the pony with the nimbleness of a cat.

"Can I wash him off?"

"'Course you can love."

Mrs Heaven allowed Tom to care for Leo. He crooned over the pony, while Leo lapped up the attention.

"How fast is he, Mrs Heaven?" asked Tom.

"He's very fast. He's great at gymkhana games and he's jumps really well."

"Jumps? You mean like when I get spooked and I jump in fright. Why's that a good thing?"

Mrs Heaven laughed. She had forgotten for a minute that Tom really didn't know anything about ponies. "Jumps means he likes leaping over obstacles, like the jumps up in the school."

"What you mean actually jump over them? While you are sitting on his back?" said Tom incredulously. "What's the point of that?"

Mrs Heaven thought for a moment, unsure of what to say. "Hmmm. You have a point there Tom. I am not really sure what the point of it is, except that it's a lot of fun."

"I'd like to gallop really fast over jumps," said Tom.

"In that case, you need to become a jockey."

"What's a jockey?"

Mrs Heaven replied: "That's the name given to people who ride in races. You may have seen them on the telly. You can have races on the flat or over jumps. Our two boys, Chilli and Elvis, both race over jumps. But they're not like the coloured show jumps in the school. They're big fences, a bit like a hedge, made of brush."

"I think I'd like to be a jockey," said Tom.

"Hold your horses love. You don't even know if you like going fast yet."

"I will. I know I will. We'll be free. Just me and Leo going fast, free as the wind," he said.

Mrs Heaven gazed at him. He was so wise for such a young child. How did he know that galloping fast would give him that sense of freedom he so craved, far removed from the hours he once spent locked away.

"It won't be long before you're galloping. Let's go back to the house and see what Ted and Emily have been up to. Maybe next time you'll ride with them."

"Er no thanks. I don't want them seeing me look stupid on a pony," he said.

"Tom you're a complete natural. Before you know it you'll be riding as well as them if not better. And you know if you ride with the others you can ride more often, because I'll have more time for you all."

"What do you mean I am a natural? A natural what? Natural boy, 'cos if that's the case it's a good job 'cos I'm not a girl am I?" he replied.

"Questions, questions," laughed Mrs Heaven. "One day, you'll know just what being a natural rider means because if you keep it up, a lot of people are going to say it to you!"

They walked back to the house together.

"Can we ride again tomorrow?" he asked.

"Let's see what the morning brings," replied Mrs Heaven.

"What do you mean by that?"

'What do I mean by that?' thought Mrs Heaven to herself before saying out loud: "If the weather is good, then yes. If not no!"

Tom felt so happy. Riding Leo had given him something he couldn't quite understand, but it felt really good, being up high, knowing that whatever he did would have a direct effect on Leo.

"If I'm nice, he's nice back. If I feel cross and angry, he can tell and doesn't want to know me. So I need to be nice," Tom said, almost to himself.

"Well yes, but you also need to let horses know who is in charge, firmly and kindly."

Chapter 5

The next day Ted and Emily quickly tacked up their ponies and led them into the school.

"Walk them around for a few minutes. It will give them some time for their muscles to warm up," called Mrs Heaven.

She turned to Tom.

"Would you like to learn how to put the bridle on?" she asked.

"OK," he replied.

Leo lowered his head obligingly. "So, you hold the bit with one hand and the rest of the bridle with the other. You place the bit in the mouth and then gently pull the bridle over his ears. It'll take a bit of practice though. Give it a go."

Tom tried a few times but couldn't get the hang of it. The bridle became a complete muddle and he gave up.

"It does take a bit of practice," repeated Mrs Heaven.

Tom said nothing. The tiniest things made him feel like he was rubbish. Mrs Heaven could see he felt troubled. I'll give the others their lesson now, and you can watch, then later we can continue where we left off yesterday, which was practising rising trot if I remember rightly," she said diverting his attention. "Unless you ride at the same time as Emily and Ted. It'll mean you'll get much more time to practice."

Tom had already thought about her words the previous day and now nodded his head reluctantly. He was so very keen to ride. Maybe the others seeing him wouldn't be as bad as he thought.

Leo nuzzled Tom with his soft white muzzle, pushing his head into his arms. For a moment Tom laid his cheek against Leo's head and everything felt fine again. 'It's just a bridle. It doesn't matter,' he told himself crossly.

"Let's go then Mrs Heaven," he said.

"It's Mandy you rascal," she replied, relieved that Tom had quickly come out from behind his barrier.

"Can I jump on while I walk by his side? Go on, you grab the reins and I'll jump up," he said.

"Certainly not young man. You can get on properly like the rest of us by using the mounting block up in the school."

Mrs Heaven was a step in front of Leo holding a long lead rein attached to his bit. Tom was walking at Leo's shoulder. Reaching up with his left arm, he grabbed a handful of mane, took one nimble leap and swung himself into the saddle sitting so lightly that Leo barely noticed. Mrs Heaven didn't notice either and continued chatting away as she watched her two children trotting around the school.

Ted was on Henry who was a strong pony with a short, thick neck, a deep girth and a stocky leg at each corner. He was slightly bigger than Leo, and nowhere near as fast, but he had a terrific jump and could clear huge show jumps and cross country fences. He had beautiful brown and white markings, which always attracted admiring gazes. Ted adored him, which was a good job, thought Mrs Heaven, otherwise he'd want to ride Leo, who was fast and agile and as quick as the point-to-pointers over short distances.

Skip was a grey and very pretty. He flicked his toes as he trotted around the school his ears pricked forward. He wasn't very brave though, and Emily had fallen off him many times when he had decided not to jump, but he was as safe as houses if there weren't any obstacles in the way.

"Come on then Tom, let's get you up and riding," said Mrs Heaven.

"No need Mandy, I'm already on!"

Mrs Heaven looked back and was shocked when she saw him sitting comfortably in the saddle.

"Thomas Pitt when you asked if you could get on, I specifically said no," she said firmly, feeling more like praising him. Even Ted and Emily, who had ridden since they were tiny, struggled to mount from the ground without using stirrups.

"I needed to save my legs, Mrs Heaven," he said grinning.

Mrs Heaven tutted: "You may be able to get on unaided, but you are not coming off the lead rein Tom, until you can control your pony adequately, so don't even ask," she said.

"Right ho, Mandy."

"And I wish you could decide whether I'm Mrs Heaven or Mandy."

"It's Mandy when I'm happy and Mrs Heaven when I'm not," he replied grinning before adding: "and I wish you could decide whether I am Thomas Pitt or plain old Tom."

"At this moment you are Thomas Pitt and every time you are Thomas Pitt it means I am in school teacher mode and therefore must be obeyed and listened to," she said in a dramatic voice, which made Tom laugh. She looked up at Tom, her kind face full of love and admiration for the skinny little boy who'd had such a rotten start in life.

Tom felt so comfortable and happy with this family, but deep inside he wondered how much longer his good fortune could last. The feelings kept bubbling to the surface, and every time they did so, he felt an ache in the pit of his stomach. 'Sooner or later,' he thought, 'Mum will want me back.' He shuddered and instinctively put his hand on Leo's neck, its warmth reassuring him.

They walked around the outside of the school together and Mrs Heaven constantly made adjustments to his position in the saddle until eventually he sat with everything in the right place. She called over to her children. "Emily and Ted, could you both go on to a circle at one end of the school? Then I'd like you to practise your walk to trot transitions." She watched as they did as she asked: "Well done Emily, that was nicely ridden. And you Ted. You are both riding really well."

She switched her attention back to Tom. "OK let's practise trotting now."

She jogged around the school, while Tom trotted, rising up and down in the saddle in time to Leo's pace.

Suddenly from the other end of the school came shrieks of laughter from Emily and guffaws from Ted. Mrs Heaven and Tom looked over to see both children sitting backwards on their ponies while attempting to ride in circles. Tom started to giggle.

Mrs Heaven yelled: "I have told you time and time again, you are not to ride backwards when I am not looking. One day you will have a nasty accident."

She marched down the school to Ted and Emily with Leo and Tom trailing behind her at the end of the long lead rope. While she wasn't looking Tom quickly spun round in the saddle so that he too was sitting backwards.

As Mrs Heaven attempted to tell off her children, Emily started to giggle. "Emily, when I am telling you off, you do not start laughing," she said in her best primary school teacher voice.

Ted put his hand up to his mouth trying to suppress a laugh.

"Ted what is wrong with you? Why is me getting cross about you riding backwards so funny?" she said, turning her head as she spoke, she saw Leo with Tom facing the wrong way.

The children started laughing uncontrollably.

Tom and Leo stopped. Tom swung his leg over the saddle to sit the right way and asked, "Everything OK Mandy?"

Mrs Heaven tried not to laugh, but the straighter she tried to keep her face, the harder it became. She started laughing uncontrollably until her tummy ached. In between fits of giggles, she managed to say: "Oh my goodness, oh my goodness. But you are naughty children. Riding backwards is not safe or correct."

The four of them took several moments to compose themselves.

"Well Tom, I guess we can try you off the lead rein, even though you've ridden a grand total of twice," Mrs Heaven said finally. "Just promise me you won't do any cowboy antics and take it one step at a time."

"Yes Mandy," said Tom, leaning forward to pat Leo.

"Let's do some sensible riding now. Go large onto the outside track."

Confused, Tom looked at Mrs Heaven and then at the children and then thought to himself, 'I guess that means puffing my cheeks out as far as they can go, pushing my tummy out and making myself big.' To do this, he let go of the reins and put his arms up over his head.

The children set off one by one. Emily sat very upright with her hands and legs in the right place. Ted adopted a less correct position, riding with his reins in one hand while the other hand rested on his knee. Mrs Heaven looked at him and was about to correct him when she glanced at Tom. By now his cheeks had gone bright red and he looked very uncomfortable.

"What on earth are you doing Tom?" she said incredulously.

He let out a huge breath.

"I've got no idea, but it's all I could think of."

"Tom, you are not being cheeky are you?"

"No Mrs Heaven, you said go large and I didn't know what else to do," he said.

"Oh Tom, we are going to have some fun. I think I'm going to need to keep a diary of all the funny things you say about things that we take for granted but which are all completely new to you. 'Go large' means to walk around the outside of the school, close to the railings, not make yourself look large."

"Oh I see. I didn't think it felt right," said Tom.

They rode for a while longer, Mrs Heaven still amazed at the ease with which Tom had taken to riding. Everything she asked him to do, he picked up immediately. She sighed thinking how lucky he was to be such a gifted and natural horseman. They finished their lesson, jumped off the ponies and took them back to the stables.

"Tom, Emily and I will see to Leo if you like. You head off with Ted for a play on the computer."

Ted untacked Henry and rubbed him down before leaving the stable yard. Tom seemed reluctant to leave.

"It's OK love, we can sort everything out. You go back to the house."

"Don't you want me here?" he asked very quietly.

"Yes of course we do, but I thought today you might like to go back with Ted to the house," said Mrs Heaven.

"But I want to help. I like it all. Even picking up the poo," Tom said.

"Then of course that's alright. You carry on and do as much work as you want," said Mrs Heaven.

"It keeps my mind busy," he said quietly to Mrs Heaven as they groomed Leo. "Stops my thinking about all the bad stuff."

Mrs Heaven looked at him sadly. It would be a long time, if ever, before he could let go of his past.

Chapter 6

That evening Mr Heaven came into the kitchen smelling of antiseptic from the veterinary practice. "Did you have a good day, everyone?" he called over to the children. They all looked up grinning.

"Tell me," he said, sensing they'd been up to something.

He walked over to Mrs Heaven and pecked her on the cheek. "All OK love?" he asked.

"I'll let the children tell you," she said giving him a quick hug.

They relayed the day's events to Mr Heaven who was highly amused: "Dearie me. It's the ponies I feel sorry for. How do they feel about being ridden backwards?"

"They don't mind at all," said Emily. "In fact I think Skip prefers it."

"I like riding forwards as fast as I can although I've only ever trotted," muttered Tom.

"Talking of which," said Mr Heaven, "I've been up at Mr Butler's racing yard today. It's a super place. There are sixty or so horses and he's invited us all over next weekend to visit. We'll meet all the horses and we'll be able to watch them work upsides on the gallop and schooling over some fences."

Emily's jaw dropped. Ted said "wow". Tom looked bemused.

"That's fab Daddy. I've always wanted to go there," shrieked Emily.

"Me to," agreed Ted.

Tom said nothing, his brow knotted in a frown.

"What's up Tom?" asked Mr Heaven.

"I don't get it," he said. "It doesn't seem right to me. You're talking nonsense. And it's cruel anyway."

Mr and Mrs Heaven looked at each in surprise.

"What do you mean love?" asked Mrs Heaven.

"Well for a start you don't do anything upsides. There's no such word. So I guess you mean upside down. Which just isn't right. And why would you work horses? What can they do that's work? 'Cos they've haven't got hands or anything like that. It's all rubbish."

Mr Heaven breathed a sigh of relief glad it was just the terminology that was upsetting Tom. "'Upsides' is when the horses go side by side up a long gallop, and 'work' means that they have to put a bit of effort into their canter. So they go quite fast. And it's thrilling to watch," he said.

"Oh my goodness," said Tom who put his hands over his cheeks trying to cover over that they had gone bright pink with embarrassment. "That's sounds like the best thing ever."

"It gets better than that Tom because we'll also watch the jockeys schooling some of the young horses over some fences."

Tom was so excited he could barely contain himself. He decided not to worry about 'schooling' horses, which also sounded a bit unlikely to him. "So I'll meet real live jockeys in all their shiny bright tops and stuff."

"They won't be wearing their bright silks, but yes, you'll get to meet them," replied Mr Heaven.

"I'm going to be a jockey one day when I'm grown up. Imagine, a life of going fast and being with ponies every single day," Tom said.

"You'd have to ride horses in those races you see on the TV, but you know you could become a jockey far sooner than that if you wanted to. There are pony races, and our local Pony Club holds a Pony Racing day once a year. You've got a way to go yet, but maybe that's something we could aim for in the autumn and you could see if you like it," said Mr Heaven.

Tom's eyes sparkled and he smiled, not a huge gaping grin, just enough for Mr and Mrs Heaven to know he was happy.

"There's another thing Tom," said Mrs Heaven. She had something important she needed to discuss with Tom, and she had been putting it off. "Your mum has asked if she can see you. It will be a supervised visit in a safe place. Would you like to see her?"

She thought she had picked the right moment, but she was wrong. There would never be a right moment. Tom's moment of happiness came crashing down around him and anxiety etched his face. Mr and Mrs Heaven hoped he would refuse to see her, knowing the painful memories they were trying to soften would came hurtling back.

He thought for a while and then said matter-of-factly. "She's my mum isn't she? So it's OK. I am happy to see her, just to say hello, no more, to check she's OK and all that. But you'll both come with me won't you?" Tom's face looked sad and he felt thrown, but he had such a good heart, he wanted to do the right thing, and if that meant seeing his mother again, then he'd do it.

"Of course we will be there. It's not for another couple of weeks so you can change your mind. Meanwhile, we've got a lot of riding to do. And we'll be fetching Chilli and Elvis in from their summer rest too. They need to start getting fit for the point-to-point season so that's something to look forward to."

That night Tom went to bed and slept fitfully. He was awake as dawn approached, a deep nagging pain in his stomach. He felt alone and frightened in that big, warm house. Over and over again he said to himself, 'Please don't take me away. Please don't take me away.' In the end, he crept out of the house to the yard to see Leo. It was still dark, but there was a bright glow on the horizon and he could just about see the path to the stable yard. Tom felt afraid. He always did when it was dark, but he knew he'd feel safe as soon as he was with Leo.

He called gently to the pony who gave a low whinny in return. 'Just keep going,' Tom told himself over and over again so that the fear didn't overwhelm him. He fumbled with Leo's door and then flopped into the straw in the corner of the stable, pulling a horse rug over him. Leo stayed close, eventually lying down beside him. Tom reached out his bony arm and nestled in close, the warmth of the pony helping keep his fears at bay. He fell into a deep sleep and, for once, the nightmares stayed away.

When the rest of the house woke, instead of panicking that he had disappeared, they headed up to the stable yard. Mrs Heaven gently roused him.

"Sorry Mrs Heaven, but I felt so scared."

"What made you scared, love?" asked Mrs Heaven clutching his hands.

"Dunno," he shrugged.

She didn't push him. He'd tell her when he was ready.

He shook off the straw and gave Leo a hug before they all walked back to the house together, Tom between Ted and Emily. He smiled at one and then the other, and Emily linked her arm through his.

"We'll always all be OK together," she said, squeezing his arm, once again not realising the magnitude of her innocent words.

Chapter 7

"Oh my, this is the best day of my life. By far," exclaimed Tom as he trotted down the beach with Mrs Heaven jogging beside him.

Leo snorted in delight when a wave broke on to the sand near his hooves. Emily and Ted trotted steadily behind, under strict instructions not to overtake Leo and Tom so that they didn't become spooked.

"Where's Dad going to be?" called Emily.

"He's on the beach at the end of the river where the sea comes in. The one we can only reach when the tide's out or by walking along the cliff path. You can't see him because of the corner, but we'll smell the sausages soon."

It was the first time Tom had ever been on a seashore, and the fact he was on Leo made it even more special. He'd heard plenty of stories about the beach, and the children he knew at his old school seemed to spend every weekend building sandcastles and playing in the waves. But his mum had never taken him, even though they lived in a city very close to the sea.

This was different to the beaches he'd read about. There was a wide shallow river that made its way to the sea, skirted on either side by sandy beaches, edged by the high cliffs. They'd reached it by a narrow lane which dropped down steeply, and there was just enough room for a handful of cars to park, so it wasn't very busy.

He looked in awe at the bright blue sea in the distance where waves tumbled onto the shore. The tide was out and the water was so shallow they could wade through it to the beach on the other side of the river. Seagulls bobbed on the water, every so often squawking to each other. There were children running, dogs barking and walkers up on the cliff park admiring the dramatic view across the South Devon coastline.

"So when Chilli and Elvis are fit, we canter them along the water's edge when the tide's out. They love coming to the beach for a play," said Mrs Heaven.

"What do you mean, fit?" asked Tom, the questions coming thick and fast now he had begun to relax into life at Hilltop House.

Mrs Heaven explained, "For a horse to race successfully, you need to build up his fitness. So you start off by walking on the roads and build up over a period of several weeks so that he can canter, and then eventually gallop, without getting out of breath. Otherwise it would be like you running in a cross country race at school, having not run for weeks."

"I'd get seriously out of breath and probably be sick," said Tom.

"That's right, so you build up the horse's fitness so that they reach their peak on the race day, just like you'd build up your own," said Mrs Heaven.

Leo ducked sideways as a wave washed over his hooves. Tom stayed relaxed and gave him a reassuring pat.

"It's alright Leo," said Tom stroking him down the neck.

"I'll just keep a lead rein on as Leo hasn't been to the beach many times and he's quite a young pony still, so it's all a bit new to him," said Mrs Heaven.

"What might he do?" asked Tom.

"He might jump about a bit. But it's only because it's unfamiliar, not because he's being naughty. As the rider, it's your job to reassure him, and ride him positively and confidently so that he doesn't think you are worried about anything."

Tom clicked his tongue, gave Leo a small nudge with his heels and said, "Come on Leo. Nothing to worry about. Just keep walking and stop worrying."

Leo broke into a steady trot his ears pricked forward as he took in the strange sights and sounds. They made their way down the beach and he suddenly skidded to an abrupt halt letting out an enormous snort.

"What have you seen Leo?" asked Tom.

"There's a terrible monster in the shape of a windbreaker about to leap out from behind that rock and gobble him up," said Mrs Heaven.

Leo's eyes were out on stalks as he looked at the strange contraption. Tom nudged him forward, quietly reassuring him and patting him down the neck.

"It's alright. It won't hurt you," said Tom and Leo sidled by blowing down his nostrils. Henry and Skip ignored it altogether having been to the beach many, many times.

"Well done Tom. That was a great bit of riding," said Mrs Heaven.

"Why? I only told him he could do it," said Tom.

"Because some children would freeze and get frightened as well, and that would cause their ponies to become more frightened. But you didn't. You kept calm and relaxed and reassured Leo that there was nothing to be fearful of."

"What, you mean some kids would be scared as well and then their ponies would think if the person on my back is scared then there is definitely something I need to be scared of? They'd get even more scared and then you'd all end up in a right jumble?"

"That's exactly right Tom," replied Mrs Heaven.

"Sometimes when I was scared of my mum, I used to wish there was someone who would help me and tell me what I'd done wrong 'cos at least then I'd know not to do it again. She would just say everything was my fault because I was bad so she had to be bad to me. That's when she punished me. But Leo doesn't think I'm bad. Otherwise he wouldn't have gone by the windbreak."

Mandy sighed. There was so much to unravel to help Tom make sense of everything that had happened to him. She took a deep breath and began. "Leo absolutely trusts you because you are a kind and good person, and because you would never hurt him and because you, in his eyes, are the leader. That trust means that when you told him it was OK to go past the windbreaker, he knew that it was. You didn't punish him for being frightened. You reassured him that there was no need to be frightened. And he trusted that. That's the secret of being a successful horseman. The animal has to trust you."

Tom interrupted. "Of course I'd never hurt Leo. Why would anyone ever hurt a pony?" he asked.

"And in the same way, no one should ever hurt a child."

"Even if they are bad?" said Tom quietly.

"You're not bad Tom," replied Mrs Heaven.

A loud voice hollered down the beach breaking their thoughts: "Sausages."

Emily kicked Skip into a canter and flew off down the beach. Henry followed on behind, his short stumpy legs going as fast as they could. Leo took a leap forward and chomped at the bit. Tom didn't waver in the saddle and instead stood lightly in his stirrups, took one hand off the rein to smooth his neck and murmured, "Steady boy, there's time enough later for a canter." Leo jig jogged for a few more strides and then relaxed. He was soon walking on a loose rein again.

Mrs Heaven kept hold of the lead rope just in case Leo decided to join the other ponies and they walked down to the beach to meet Mr Heaven. He was ready with sausage rolls and handed them to the children and then poured Mrs Heaven a cup of tea.

"All OK in the pony ranks?" he asked.

"Brilliant Dad, thanks," said Emily.

"I think I'll unclip this rope," said Mrs Heaven to Tom who nodded eagerly in agreement. He felt a bit silly being attached to a lead. Mandy then joined her husband and helped hand out the sausages. Tom turned Leo to face the sea and sat mesmerised as the waves crashed to and fro onto the shore. One after the other they rolled onto the yellow sands, breaking with white crests which frothed up onto the beach. Leo stood transfixed, his ears pricked forwards and his deep brown eyes staring out at sea.

Tom bent down and whispered. "Are you ready Leo?" The pony responded by tossing his head and suddenly they were galloping across the sands to the waves.

Mrs Heaven screamed. "Tom, Tom. Come back. Emily, Ted don't you go too. He can't control Leo. He doesn't know how to stop. Jim do something. He'll fall off and hurt himself."

Mr Heaven looked into the distance as Tom reached the waves and saw him gently steady Leo to a trot, then nudge him forward to splash along the water's edge, Leo high-stepping through the water.

"He's alright, look Mandy. Look he has complete control. And what's the worse that can happen? He'll fall off into the sand and have a soft landing and Leo will come back to his friends Skip and Henry."

Mrs Heaven's worried frown relaxed and as she watched Tom coaxing Leo into the water she realised she had nothing to worry about.

"Mum, why can't we gallop down to the beach? It's not fair. We ride much better than Tom and you've never let us do that," moaned Emily.

Ted agreed. "Yeah Mum. It's not fair. Why can't we gallop too?"

Mrs Heaven looked at her husband who gave the slightest of nods.

"Go on then, off you go and its yes, not yeah, Ted. Speak properly," she said her voice trailing off as Ted and Emily cantered their ponies towards the water's edge.

Tom looked at them and grinned. Leo became agitated standing still as he watched the ponies tearing towards him so Tom pushed him into trot. He quickly settled, feeling happier moving forwards.

"S'funny Leo," remarked Tom to the pony. "You're taking all

your comfort from me today, instead of the other way around!"

Ted and Emily caught up and they splashed through the waves together. The ponies high-stepped and huge plumes of water soaked the children.

"Shall we gallop back to Mum and Dad?" shouted Emily.

"Actually no," replied Tom.

"Scaredy cat," goaded Emily.

"I'm not scared at all. I'm just thinking of Leo. He's always so calm and this beach stuff has sparked him right up. If I go racing back up there, every time he comes to the beach, he'll think that's what he's supposed to do."

Leo turned his head to nudge Tom's toe as if he was agreeing with him.

"I still think you're scared Tom. Too scared to gallop," Emily whined.

Tom wanted to kick on and prove her wrong. Instead he patted Leo's neck and quietly said: "I don't care what you think and if you think I'm scared, whatever."

Ted butted in. "Emily, leave Tom alone and let him do what he likes. What does it matter? He galloped here didn't he?"

Emily sulked. She walked behind the boys and then refused to speak when they reached her parents.

"Well that looked like fun," said Mr Heaven. "But you know Tom, that wasn't great horsemanship because you could have caused a problem for Skip and Henry who may have wanted to join you. Luckily they're used to ponies galloping around through years in the Pony Club."

"He's scared anyway. He wouldn't gallop back," said Emily.

Tom ignored her and stared at Leo's mane. Emily expected him to shout back, like her brother would. But he looked away, biting his lower lip hard. He hated being teased. It made him feel like everyone was watching him and he'd rather be invisible.

Chapter 8

The sun was feeling its way into the morning sky and a soft grey mist hung over the dewy fields. Mr Heaven's Land Rover made its way up the lane and away from Hilltop House. The children sat side by side in the back seat and, stifling a yawn, Emily laid her head on Ted's shoulder. She wasn't trying to be affectionate. She was trying to annoy her big brother.

"Get off Emily," Ted said shoving her into Tom.

Tom ignored her and instead stared quietly out of the window watching the fields and woodland fly by and imagining huge horses with jockeys perched on their backs galloping as fast as the wind.

"Now I want you to be good and polite and most of all quiet. No screeching, no squawking and definitely no squabbling. Mr Butler is one of my best clients and I don't want him thinking I've raised a bunch of hooligans," lectured Mr Heaven.

"And do put your hand over your mouth when you yawn, Emily," said Mrs Heaven. "Not everyone wants to see a mouthful of teeth, especially first thing in the morning."

Mr Heaven continued, "When we get there, you are to be polite to Mr Butler." Be sure you all shake his hand if he offers it."

"Yes Dad," chorused Emily and Ted looking at each other and raising their eyebrows pulling faces.

"Can we just get there now? We do know how to behave you know. Your years of nagging haven't completely gone to waste," said Ted.

Mrs Heaven glanced at her husband raising her eyes upwards and Mr Heaven winked in response. "Glad to hear it Ted. Best behaviour all round then."

After winding along the country lanes for what seemed an age, they arrived at a large entrance where a slate plaque pinned on a stone pillar declared in fancy gold writing that they had arrived at Hall Farm Racing Stables.

"This is it Dad. We're here," exclaimed Emily. "We're here Ted. We're here Tom," she said pinching them both.

"Get off Emily," said Ted thumping her.

"Ow," she shrieked and was about to start howling when she heard Tom very quietly say: "Emily, you asked for that."

"No I did not," she replied sulkily, but she didn't howl.

The drive swept down towards a large red brick house that had stone steps leading up to an imposing white door with huge horse head statues made of grey granite on either side of it.

"Follow me troops," said Mr Heaven parking the Land Rover and jumping out.

He walked along the wide gravel path that skirted around the side of the house to the back where a row of stables stood a stone's throw from the kitchen window. There were only eight stables. Their top doors were pinned back and decorated with plaques announcing the names of various famous races the inhabitants had won. Out of each stable, except one, peered the fine head of a thoroughbred horse.

Instead of noticing the beautiful horses that stared intently at them with their ears pricked forward expectantly, Emily started whining. "But Dad, I thought you said there were sixty horses." Disappointment was etched across her face.

"There are at least sixty horses Emily. This here is the top yard where the best horses live. Each one of these horses has won a big race, and you may even have seen them on TV," said Mr Heaven. "This is West is Best," he continued, walking towards the first stable. A handsome horse the colour of a polished conker with a white stripe down the middle of his face nuzzled his hand gently. "He's a hurdler and he doesn't like the big fences. Then here's Bobby Blue Shoes. He's a staying chaser." Mr Heaven carried on, oblivious to his children's blank stares and clearly in awe of the horses.

"What's Dad on about?" Emily asked Ted. He shrugged his shoulders in response and walked towards one of the horses who sniffed his hand as if it were a delicate flower.

Tom felt like he'd been transported to another world. 'I can't believe I am here,' he said to himself, thinking that at any moment he would wake up from a wonderful dream.

Suddenly a tall man appeared. He had a sizeable stomach and was wearing bright pink corduroy trousers, a red jumper and a navy waistcoat. He strolled towards them and as he did so he roared, "Hullo Jim."

At the sound of his voice, all the horses whinnied and he went to each one in turn scratching them on their necks and cooing after them before turning his attention back to Mr and Mrs Heaven and the children.

"So pleased to see you all. You must be Emily, you're Ted and you're Tom. I'm Mr Butler. Welcome to Hall Farm Racing Stables."

He offered his hand first to Tom who stared at it blankly.

After a second or two Mr Butler turned and held it out to Emily and Ted who both shock shook it gently, up and down. Tom flushed a deep crimson colour and kept his eyes firmly fixed on the ground.

"Follow me then," he called before bending down and whispering to Tom: "And don't worry about the handshake. It just bonds a friendship, and I do hope we'll be friends," he said with kindness in his voice.

Tom looked up at him nervously. "Th-th-thank you, Mr Butler," he stuttered, completely awe struck that this great man was actually talking to him.

"So, Emily, Ted, Tom I see your dad has already introduced you to some of the horses," he said.

"Well, yes, but he wasn't very good at explaining things. He just seemed to drift off into a world of his own talking about hurdles and big fences," said Ted.

"He's not my dad," muttered Tom, but no one heard him or at least if they did, they ignored him.

"Your father," carried on Mr Butler carried on, "as well as being an exemplary vet, is also rather a fan of jump racing, as you well know if you'd taken any notice of those two fine point-to-pointers you have. Have you ever heard of the Cheltenham Gold Cup?"

"Yes," replied Ted. "I've seen it on the TV. Isn't it the best race a horse can win?"

"It's one of the best, and one that every racehorse owner aspires to win, well either that or the Grand National. Only the very best horses are capable of winning it, they have to have a lot of stamina to keep galloping for three miles. Plus, they have to be really brave to jump the big fences. This horse, Bobby Blue Shoes, won the Cheltenham Gold Cup last season, and we'll be going for the same race again with him this season."

Bobby hung his head out over the stable door with an expression that begged for attention. Tom duly obliged and stroked him down the side of the face.

"To his left is West is Best who has won the Champion Hurdle twice, a remarkable achievement. But show him a fence and he goes to pieces. I mean he won't jump them not that his legs fall off or anything unfortunate like that," said Mr Butler quickly, realizing realising the children were taking him at his word.

Emily giggled: "That would be so weird if he fell into pieces like a jigsaw puzzle. You'd need so much glue to stick him back together."

Mr Butler interrupted her saying, "This is the top yard, and through that alley there is the main yard where the rest of the horses live."

He led the way to a large stable yard with a square of grass in the middle and loose boxes along all four sides. There was an arched entrance at the far end that led to myriad barns, cottages and paddocks. The whole place was alive with activity with people coming in and out of stables, pushing wheelbarrows, carrying saddles and bridles and generally being very busy.

"And this is the Hall House Racing Stables team," said Mr Butler gesturing with his hands.

"In ten minutes the second lot will pull out, and we'll head up to the gallops to watch them work. But first of all come and meet Ben Steed and Mickey O'Leary, two of the best jockeys in the land."

They walked towards a room with 'Lads' Canteen' written across the top of the doorway. Inside a bunch of young people were devouring pieces of toast and downing cups of tea while cracking jokes and laughing.

"Guv'nor's coming," they heard one of them shout and the whole group quickly grabbed their crash caps and started to walk in different directions to the horses they were about to ride.

"Why is it called lads' canteen?, Mr Butler," ventured Ted. "There are girls as well as boys."

"Male or female, you're a lad in racing," Mr Butler replied before shouting, "Ben, Mickey, here a minute will you lads."

Two tall, skinny young men marched over. Tom couldn't help thinking that they wore the oddest clothes he had ever seen: skin-tight leather boots came up to their knees, baggy blue breeches that looked like elephant ears adorned their thighs and short waterproof navy blue jackets with 'Hall Farm Racing Stables' embroidered in gold across the back covered their slight bodies.

Ben beamed as he approached: "Hello guys. Welcome to Hall Farm Racing Stables. It's a grand place here, with some of the best horses you could hope to find. Thinking of being a jockey are you?" he asked no one in particular.

Tom looked away. He wanted to speak, but the words just wouldn't come out. Ted said, "Maybe." Emily said nothing. She'd seen jockeys on the TV and thought they were the bravest people that walked the planet. Now she was actually standing next to one, she was speechless, which was unusual for Emily.

"Well," continued Ben who had such a huge smile it seemed to stretch from ear to ear. "Let me introduce you to Mickey. Number two jockey to me."

"So," said Mickey offering his hand.

This time Tom knew to shake it up and down. "Well that's a good enough hand shake for a small boy like yourself," said Mickey with a wink.

"What?" asked Tom.

Mickey repeated himself.

"'Scuse me but I don't know what you're saying."

"That's your Irish accent, Mickey," laughed Ben.

"So how long have you been riding?" Ben asked Tom. Finding the courage to speak, Tom said, "W-w-well only a few times. With Mr and Mrs Heaven. I haven't got my own pony. But I live at Hilltop House, for now anyway," he finished very quietly.

Hearing the angst in his voice, Emily's tender side erupted to the surface. She protectively linked her arm through his and her words tumbled out: "Actually, he's always going to live with us. Because we all really like him. He doesn't fight with me like my brother and he's brilliant at mucking out. And he can ride a pony backwards too," she said.

"Well that's a good enough reason isn't it?" laughed Ben.

Tom smiled shyly, grateful for Emily's kind words.

Ted kicked her. "Emily don't be silly. He's not with us 'cos he mucks out. It's 'cos his mum is ill."

Mrs Heaven interrupted, "Quiet you two. So Ben, who are you going to be riding today?"

"With four other lads, we'll work six up the gallops first and then Mickey and I will school two horses over fences. I'll be on a horse called Francome, and trust me when I say he'll win the Queen Mother one day."

"That's a top race, kids," said Mrs Heaven and then asked, "What about you Mickey?"

He replied, very concisely, "Marco Polo and Dear Daisy."

"That's such a cool name, Dear Daisy. My pony is called Skip and he's grey and he doesn't like jumping," gabbled Emily.

"Kick him on, shout 'hup' and you'll soon get him over," said Ben.

"I would never, ever kick my pony. If he doesn't want to jump, that's fine by me," Emily retorted.

"Is that so?" said Ben. "But jumping is such a fine thing to do. Fills you with some kind of a buzz. Anyway, we'll be off now then. See you in a bit."

"Later," added Mickey and they both ambled off towards the stables.

"Dad, why do they talk so weirdly?" asked Emily.

"It's cool. It's not weird," said Ted.

"I could hardly understand a thing, other than jumping is a buzz," said Tom.

Mr Butler clapped his hands loudly together, making the children jump, and then said, "Wait right here and I will come and pick you up."

He disappeared around the corner and soon returned driving what looked like a golf buggy. "Gator, meet the Heavens, Heavens meet the Gator. All aboard. I'll need to shout over this noisy engine, but listen in." He trundled the buggy out of the yard, then put his foot down as he approached the gateway into the fields. Beside the gallop, which seemed to be made of sand, was a narrow track.

"So, the horses will come in through that gate over there," he said pointing to a gap in the hedge. They'll circle around a few times in that big space and then set off slowly up this gallop, which is seven furlongs in total. You can see where it sweeps up following the contour of the hill. They'll pull up at the top.

"We'll go half way up, by which time the horses that are working will be going at some lick so you'll really get a sense of their power and speed."

He put his foot flat to the metal and they jerked and jolted along side the gallop until he stopped half way, scrambled out and climbed up a ladder to a viewing platform, which was raised high above the ground.

"Best view in the country here. Come on up," he shouted.

Emily climbed up, followed by Ted.

"Actually, can I stay here please? It's just I'd like to be as close to the horses as possible. Hear them breathe and see their muscles," said Tom.

"'Course you can lad, but perhaps your mum and dad should stay down with you," called Mr Butler from his perch.

Tom was about to say, "They're not my mum and dad," but stopped as Mrs Heaven put a comforting arm around his shoulders. Even if they weren't his real mum and dad, it was as good as, Tom thought to himself.

Chapter 9

"They're coming," called Mr Butler. "Now keep quiet and still. We don't want to spook the horses."

He trained his binoculars on six black specks, which rapidly grew larger as they approached. They could hear the horses' hooves thundering on the gallop and as they came nearer, they could hear them breathing hard as they strained against the taut reins. They could see the jockeys standing in their stirrups, poised over the horse's backs, their hands quite still against either side of the withers, their weight perfectly balanced as they came up the gallop, one behind the other.

'Oh wow, oh wow,' said Tom to himself over and over again.

Ben Steed was in front on a huge bay horse whose nostrils were flared and whose nose was tucked in close to his chest as he tried to quicken the pace. Ben kept very still in the saddle. "Steady fella. No need to waste your energy. Just settle into the rhythm."YES

"Oh my, that's so fast," shouted Emily trying hard not to wave her arms in delight.

"That's a very slow canter for these chaps. They'll come a bit quicker next time," said Mr Butler.

As they passed, Tom felt the air rush by and turned with it to watch their progress as they neared the top of the hill.

One by one the horses slowed to a walk and then, turning, came jogging back down the hill towards the platform.

"Upsides next time, quicken at two so that you're going half speed by three for two furlongs," called Mr Butler.

"Yes guv'nor," replied Ben who stood in his stirrups and let his horse jog down the hill keeping his weight off his back. "This is Bogwash by the way kids, and Mickey is on Dear Daisy," he shouted.

"Well that's a name and a half," said Mr Heaven.

"Ah, there's a bit of a tale behind that name," explained Mr Butler. "You see, he was born in Ireland, near a bog, a wee bit early, so his dam, that's mother, was out in a field, rather than in a stable, and Paddy Healey, who bred him, went splat, face first into the mud as they brought him in. 'You'll want a bog wash now,' his wife said, and the name stuck. We call him Boggy, not Bogey, kids, Boggy."

Ted joked: "Seems a bit odd to me having a loo out in a field."

"Not a loo, Ted, a bog is mud that you sink into," corrected Emily primly.

The horses had arrived at the bottom of the gallop. Even from this distance, they could see how they jigged and snatched at their reins, eager to get going again. Ben and Mickey jumped off together, their horses cantering side by side. At the two-furlong marker, they quickened and by the time they arrived at the platform they were going at a gallop.

The horses' hooves seemed merely to kiss the ground as they thundered by, breathing hard, foamy sweat dripping from their powerful bodies. Ben and Mickey were absolutely motionless, like puppets pinned to the horses' saddles. Tom was mesmerized mesmerised by the apparent effortlessness of it all and wished he could be on a horse too.

"It must feel like they are flying," he said.

"It certainly gives you a very special feeling," agreed Mr Heaven.

"Can Leo go that fast?"

"He's a quick pony over a short distance, and he's definitely faster than Skip and Henry, but he wouldn't be able to keep it up for long like these chaps," Mr Heaven said.

"It looks brill. Can I have a go? With my stirrups up short and my legs all bent."

"One day," Mr Heaven said. "You just need a bit more practice first."

"In the autumn, then, at the pony race?" Tom persisted.

"Maybe," said Mr Heaven who seemed distracted as he watched the horses surging away up the hill.

To Tom, Mr Heaven's apparent lack of interest in the pony race spelt trouble. He went very quiet, forgetting about the excitement of galloping horses. His thoughts were elsewhere as his stomach started churning and fear rose from the pit of his stomach. He tried hard to control it. He told himself that he was being silly, that Mr Heaven didn't mean anything by saying "maybe" and that he would still be going pony racing. But the worst thoughts kept bubbling to the surface, and he couldn't stop himself from thinking that Mr Heaven had said maybe because he knew he was going back to his mother.

"I need to get out of here. I need to go," he blurted out, and took off running down the hill, tears streaming down his face.

"Mum, mum Mum what's wrong with Tom?" yelled Emily from the tower.

Mrs Heaven had been as entranced as everyone by the horses and hadn't noticed Tom dashing down the hill as fast as his legs could carry him.

"Are you OK Tom? What's wrong? Tom come back," she shouted.

But Tom was already approaching the bottom of the gallop.

"I'm so sorry Mr Butler. I don't know what's got into him," she called over her shoulder as she ran after him.

Before she reached the bottom, she heard the sound of hooves behind her, and stopped running as Ben swept by, followed by Mickey. As they neared the gate, Ben leapt off Bogwash and threw his reins to Mickey. Breaking into a run, he chased after Tom, who was making for the hedge the other side of the gate, his hoody pulled down over his head, sobs wracking his body.

Mr Butler was the last down from the platform. He jumped into his buggy and drove down to Mr Heaven, Emily and Ted who were half way down the hill by now.

"Hop in. "If anyone can sort out what's up with him, Ben can," he said reassuringly.

They made their way to the bottom of the gallop. Mr Heaven got out of the buggy and began pacing up and down, holding his chin with his hand. Mrs Heaven watched him but stood close to her children, knowing they would be as worried about Tom as she and her husband.

"It is often the smallest little things that can cause anxiety in a foster child." Mr Butler said. "As you know, Dixie and I have fostered several children over the years, and we get there in the end with all of them."

"I do hope so Mr Butler," said Mrs Heaven. "We think the world of him. He's a good kid."

"And he's really cool to have around," said Emily.

"I can tell that and he seems to have fitted in well. At least you know his passion and that'll always help. Show him a horse and he'll be fine," said Mr Butler.

On the other side of the hedge Tom had pushed himself as far into the leafy bushes as he could, even though the brambles scratched him. Pangs of loneliness pierced his thoughts like ice rods and he kept telling himself that nobody in the world cared for him. That's what Mum always said, he thought, and she was right. But all the while, a tiny nagging doubt was growing in his mind until, finally, it began to win the battle. As much as he told himself he was worthless and the Heavens were eventually going to send him back to his mother, he couldn't help thinking that they really did genuinely like him. By the time Ben reached him, he was already feeling better. Ben quietly sat down beside him. He reached gently into the hedge and took one of Tom's hands between his. He held it there for a few moments, letting Tom feel the comfort of another human being.

"So Tom, what's bugging you?" he asked eventually.

"I don't know. I just..." said Tom, lost for words.

"You can tell me Tom," said Ben.

"It's just sometimes...I get scared. And I think I'm going back there, to Mum," he said.

"And what made you start thinking that when you were on the gallops just now," ?" asked Ben gently.

Tom felt like he couldn't get his words out, and if he did, they'd come out wrong and he'd sound more stupid than ever.

"Look Tom, whatever it is, it's better out than in. Trust me I know. Let the bad thoughts out, just like you would a burp."

Tom looked at him curiously.

"You know what I mean. When you want to burp, you always feel better after you've let it out," Ben said, trying to explain himself.

Amusement flickered across Tom's face.

"Well it's true isn't it?" said Ben. "You always feel relief after a good old burp, and it's the same if you let the bad thoughts out!"

Tom muttered into his hoodie: "Up there, I thought Mr Heaven wanted to send me back to Mum, but I don't really think he does."

"I know for a fact he doesn't want to send you back. Why on earth would he? But anyway, I'd be interested to know what on earth brought on those feelings."

Tom tried to explain himself. "It's just that he said 'maybe'..."

"So you think that because he said the word 'maybe', that's it and you're off back to your mother," said Ben in a matter-of-fact way.

"Well no...not really...sort of. He said 'maybe' when I asked if I could ride in a pony race in the autumn. And 'maybe', in my house, always meant no."

Ben interrupted: "At which point did he say this?"

"As the horses galloped by."

"How did you feel when the horses were galloping by?"

"Out of this world. Like I was in another place. It was awesome," said Tom.

"Do you think that maybe Mr Heaven felt the same?" asked Ben.

"Yeah, he would have felt proud of those horses, 'cos I know he loves them."," agreed Tom.

"Exactly. He was enjoying watching the horses. Tom I know for certain that Mr and Mrs Heaven consider you part of their family. Even better than that, I also know that you are a born natural in the saddle. With any luck you'll be pony racing soon and if you take to that, maybe you could be doing exactly what I do one day. Earning a living out of riding horses. I've already said to Mr Butler and Mr Heaven that I would be delighted to help you, including riding upsides on the gallop to watch up close how you ride."

"Do you mean that? Is that what they said?" asked Tom.

"Of course I mean that. Why wouldn't I? None of us here are in the habit of saying things we don't mean. Come back with me, and it will all be fine, I promise."

"I can't. They'll all hate me for being so stupid and running off." A lump rose in Tom's throat as he tried to fend off the tears.

"Tom, listen to me. No one here hates you. You're a kid and the things you've seen and the things you've been through are just not right. Mr and Mrs Heaven know that, I know that, the Butlers know that and Mickey knows that. You're a good kid, and you deserve happiness, and you need to trust me when I say that's exactly what you're going to get."

Tom's insides felt tight. The only place he'd ever felt safe and warm was with the Heavens. Now Ben, a jockey, and already his hero, was trying to help him too. He still couldn't help wondering why anyone would want to be nice to him, but he decided at that moment, that he would let them. So he gave the slightest of nods. Ben immediately stood up and, grabbing Tom's other hand, pulled him out of the hedge and onto his feet.

"Now wipe those tears away because it's all going to be fine."

"And you're really sure that I'm not going back to Mum, and that I will get to ride up the gallops?" Tom whispered.

"I'm more than sure. I am positive, although there's a little matter of giving your riding a little bit more polish at home first. But that will come with time and plenty of practice," said Ben, and scooping Tom up he gave him a fireman's lift over his shoulder and carried him through the gate. "You're as light as a feather Tom. Just right for being a jockey one day!" he laughed.

They found Mr Butler, Mr and Mrs Heaven, Emily and Ted still standing at the bottom of the gallops. Apart from Mr Butler, who had a knowing look about him, all the others were distracted with worry and Mr Heaven was still pacing up and down.

Mickey was walking around in a circle on Dear Daisy, leading Bogwash. It was as if they were doing some curious kind of dance. As Ben lowered Tom to the ground, giving everyone the thumbs up, he started chuckling: "Tom, will you just look at that. They've been so worried for you, they've created a new dance where they you pace around in random circles."

Tom looked up and nearly started to giggle, and then thought better of it when he saw how worried everyone looked. Mrs Heaven gestured to the others to stay where they were. She hurried over and gave Tom a big hug, before grabbing his hand and leading him towards the Gator.

Tom glanced at everyone then stared hard into the ground: "Sorry," he said meekly.

"Not sure what you are sorry for, but there's no time to talk about things now," bustled Mr Butler. "Do that later. Ben and Mickey, you need to jump on Francome and Marco Polo and pop them over the chase fences. I think Dear Daisy and Boggy are nicely cooled down now so you can take them back to the lads in the yard and bring the other two up to the schooling ground."

Mr and Mrs Heaven gave him a grateful look of thanks and they all clambered back into the Gator for another bone-trembling ride up to the schooling fences. Tom sat between Emily and Ted. Emily leant over and gave him a kiss. Ted thumped him hard on the arm. Tom didn't know whether to blush at Emily's affection or thump Tom back. Either way, he felt wonderful and it wasn't long before his beautiful grin lit up his face again.

The schooling ground was at the top of the gallops. It was a huge space with lines of fences at various heights ranging from poles barely off the ground to towering brush fences.

"Come and take a look kids. We've a while before Francome and Marco Polo arrive," said Mr Butler squeezing through the small door of the Gator. "So this is where we teach the horses to jump at speed after they've learned the basics in our huge sand school beyond the woods there."

"We've got a sand school," interrupted Emily. "Do you remember we said that Tom's brill at riding backwards? Well that's where we do it."

"Riding backwards is no good at all for aspiring jockeys," said Mr Butler peering at Tom who blushed bright red.

He walked over to the large fence that looked like it was made of closely packed branches, held together by two bright orange poles. Tom, Ted and Emily followed him. They couldn't see over it, it was so big, and it seemed just as wide.

"They don't really jump these do they? They are massive," said Ted.

"They certainly do, but they approach them at a fair pace, take them in their stride and sail over. This orange board here helps them to judge where to take off, and this padded pole above it stops them hurting their legs if they touch the fence. Some horses, during a race, will take off as far away as the end of these white wings. It is quite incredible," said Mr Butler.

By this time, Tom had forgotten all about his troubles. He was very impressed at the thought of jumping these huge fences; he didn't quite believe it was possible.

"But why would a horse want to jump something so big," ?" he said, his voice barely above a whisper.

"They love it, that's why. Comes naturally to them. You'll see for yourself in a few moments."

Just as Mr Butler said that, they heard the distant sounds of horses' hooves pounding up the hill and they saw Marco Polo and Francome, their long strides steadily eating up the ground.

"That's the best sound in the world," said Tom, animated once more.

"You're right there lad," said agreed Mr Butler. "But you wait until you hear it on a racecourse. Now that really is the best sound ever."

Ben and Mickey pulled up at the top of the gallop, and then trotted their horses to the schooling field, bringing them to a halt next to Mr Butler. Francome stood quite still, the sun making his damp black coat glisten. He gazed into the distance; his ears pricked forward, his huge brown eyes focused on some far off object. He was a powerhouse of energy, ready to surge away, and he suddenly swung his quarters around, eager to get going again.

"Steady lad," said Ben, letting him walk round in a circle.

Marco Polo was smaller, a deep chestnut colour with a small white star in the centre of his forehead and an unusual flash of white in his tail. Mickey trotted him on, standing in his stirrups while murmuring to him in soothing tones.

"Twice up over the smaller of the chases, upsides. Get a bit of pace into it the second time up," called Mr Butler.

They could hear the horses blowing as they approached the first fence and, without seeming to alter their pace, flew over the brush, landing in a gallop and then meeting the second obstacle. Their front legs lifted off the ground and they tucked them up as they jumped, just brushing the top of the birch, and then they landed on one front leg, the other following close behind, before galloping away.

The children stood very still, lost for words. "That looks like a real buzz," said Ted.

"I could see their tummies as they jumped. It looked like they were space rockets when they took off," Emily said.

Mr and Mrs Heaven nodded in appreciation at the athleticism of the horses.

"One more time," shouted Mr Butler and Ben and Mickey galloped towards the fences again, this time going a bit quicker. Again they met both fences perfectly, soaring through the air in an arc shape. Ben and Mickey barely moved, and crouched low in their saddles allowing the reins to run through their hands so that they didn't hinder the horses as they stretched their necks out. As they leapt, silence, and then their thundering hooves echoed from the hilltop again. Pulling up, Ben and Mickey patted their horses' necks and then jogged back to Mr Butler.

"Well done. They don't need to do anymore so take them back to the stables now," he said.

He looked very happy as he turned to Tom and the Heavens and said, "Now that's what I call a decent couple of racehorses."

They all nodded in agreement but they were lost for words. The spirit and energy of the horses had left them speechless.

"Cat got your tongues," laughed Mr Butler as he looked at the line of people who were still standing with their mouths slightly open. "I have to say, I've seen a few things in my life, but never before a family of five trying to look like goldfish. Come on then let's go back to the house for a cup of tea and a slice of something nice. I think Dixie might have made my favourite chocolate cake!"

Chapter 10

Mr Butler parked the Gator by the back door of the house, and as he climbed out, the seven horses in the top yard whinnied in unison. It was the sweetest, most welcoming sound Tom had ever heard.

"Hello boys. It'll soon be time for your afternoon in the paddocks," Mr Butler called. The horses tossed their heads sending their silky manes cascading in different directions.

"Mr Butler. Do you think they understand you?" Tom asked nervously.

"Absolutely, my boy. They certainly know the word 'paddock'. It's all part of their routine and going out there keeps them fresh and sweet. Every afternoon, come rain or shine, they go out in the fields for a play, a roll, and for some Dr Green."

"Who's Dr Green?" chirped Emily.

"Dr Green is the best medicine for any horse. It's grass!" Mr Butler said.

They followed him through the large white door that led into a huge kitchen. It had a grey flagstone floor, and in the middle stood an enormous table covered in a pink tablecloth dotted with white spots. Hundreds of photographs adorned the walls with barely a gap between them, and the shelves on the dresser were laden with trophies of every shape, colour and description.

"I see you are all doing your goldfish impression again," laughed Mr Butler as the children traipsed in, followed by Mr and Mrs Heaven, in awe at their surroundings. "Sit your selves down and let's find that chocolate cake," he continued disappearing through a door. He soon came back with the biggest cake Tom had ever seen. Tom loved cake. Before he went to live with the Heavens, he'd hardly ever tasted it, but he had quickly developed a sweet tooth and his mouth started watering as he eyed it hungrily.

Mr Butler passed around some plates, found a knife and started to cut generous slices, calling to his wife as he did so. Dixie appeared and she was not what Emily, Ted or Tom expected at all. It would be fair to say that Mr Butler seemed a shade old-fashioned with his outlandish clothes, and bustling ways. Dixie, however, was extraordinarily beautiful and right up to the minute, with a mane of long golden locks and huge blue eyes. She wore dark blue breeches, a pair of fluffy slippers and a checked shirt.

Tom could not stop looking at her. 'I think I've met an angel,' he said to himself, as Dixie went up to each of the children in turn and gave them a warm handshake.

"How lovely to meet you all," she said smiling. "I've heard so much about you."

Mr Butler walked towards the biggest picture on the wall. Taken in a crowded winners' enclosure, it showed a racehorse with a rider who was punching the air. He said proudly said, "This is Dixie here, after she won a hurdle race at the Festival. It was a tough race, but she beat the best of them. Best female jockey there's ever been, in my opinion."

Dixie didn't look tough enough to be a jockey. She was so tall and willowy; she looked more like a model. "That was a long time ago," she smiled. "Although I still ride out two horses every day, in between looking after our brood of kids, who, by the way, are outside playing on the climbing frame, except Henry, who's up in his room on the computer."

She placed a huge pot of tea on the table and handed out mugs. "I'm guessing you kids would rather have some juice," she said and they nodded in agreement.

"What's it like being a jockey?" asked Emily.

"There's nothing quite like it for the thrill it gives you, but you have to be fearless, because as soon as any nerves start to creep in, your horse will pick up on it, and he'll know. I loved it while I did it, but I started to worry, and that's when I retired, before I got broken up in a fall," said Dixie.

"You mean you actually broke bones?" ventured Emily.

"That's right. I did have a few falls, but was lucky enough to just to break my collar bone a couple of times," she replied.

"You call that lucky," laughed Ted.

"So," said Dixie changing the subject, "I hear you all love riding."

The children nodded eagerly, never for a moment taking their gaze off this lovely woman who had rapidly ascended to the top of the pedestal, knocking off Ben and Mickey in the process.

"Emily would like to do more showing, and Ted likes going hunter trialling. Tom wants to ride in a pony race, so that's our aim for the autumn," said Mrs Heaven.

Tom nodded while Dixie said, "That's fabulous. Some of the best riders in the country started off in pony races. It's the perfect way to learn all about being a jockey."

Mr Butler thrust a huge pile of photographs on the table. "Dive in everyone. There are some wonderful moments in those photographs. It will give you a taste of the magic of horseracing."

The children grabbed a handful each, and studied them enthusiastically while Mr and Mrs Heaven watched them, enthralled. This trip to their friends' racing stables was turning out to be a huge success. There was a photograph of West is Best flying up the hill in the Gold Cup, another of Bobby Blue Shoes jumping a hurdle in the Champion, his front legs tucked up, his hind legs trailing behind him. His jockey, Ben, was bent so low, his nose was virtually touching his mane. You could see the raised veins in Bobby Blue Shoes' neck, his nostrils were flared and his ears were slightly back, as he put all his power and energy into jumping the hurdle at speed. In another photograph, Dixie stood on a podium wearing pink and blue silks, white breeches and shiny black boots. Her long hair fell around her waist and she held aloft an enormous trophy.

They leafed through the photographs one by one mesmerized by the wonderful images. Suddenly they heard the sound of horses' hooves so loud it was as if they were coming into the kitchen. Everyone looked up to where Best Is West and Bobby Blue Shoes were peering in through the open window, dressed from ears to tail in thick outdoor rugs. Their lads waved at the children who waved back giggling.

"They are off for their play in their paddocks," said Mr Butler walking over to give the horses a polo each.

"This has got to be the coolest place on earth," said Emily.

"One day I'd love to work somewhere like this," said Tom.

"Well young man, when you are just a little bit older, come along during your holidays and ride out. I think you'd be a very valuable addition to the team," said Mr Butler.

"I second that. You'd have a super time," agreed Dixie.

Mr and Mrs Heaven both winked at the Butlers, as if they had some kind of secret pact between them, while the children went back to the photographs.

"Right well, we mustn't take up anymore of the Butlers' time," said Mr Heaven scraping his chair back.

"Before you all go, let's just take a walk around the main yard. Then you can get to know the horses," suggested Mr Butler.

"That's a wonderful idea. Come along troops.," Mr Heaven replied.

They followed Mr Butler and one by one he told them the names of the horses and the races they had won. As they approached the far end, Tom noticed a horse who stood with his head hung low over the door looking very unhappy.

"He looks so sad," he said very quietly.

"Well observed Tom. He's called Mr Happy, but he's anything but and we can't work out why," said Mr Butler opening the stable door and putting on Mr Happy's headcollar.

Mr Heaven followed him into the stable and gave him a quick examination. "His skin feels good, his breathing is good, his temperature is normal and his heart rate is normal. Everything looks fine to me," he said.

Mr Butler shook his head. "It's baffling us," he said as they walked out, closing the stable door behind them.

Mr Happy put his head back over the door and looked so sad it brought tears to Emily's eyes. "I think he hates being a race horse," she said.

"Well that did cross our minds, but he is phenomenal in his races and as soon as he's on the racecourse he lights up," said Mr Butler.

They all stood watching Mr Happy, who looked so glum it made them all feel sad. The horse to his left threw back his ears and glared at him, just as the horse in the stable on the other side appeared over his door and did exactly the same thing.

"I think he's unhappy because he doesn't like his neighbours," Tom said so quietly the others barely heard him.

"What did you say?" asked Mr Butler.

"Those other horses. They really don't like him. That's what's making him so unhappy. He doesn't like the horses either side of him."

Mr Butler stared at Tom, stared back at the horses and then looked at Tom again. Slapping Tom on the back, which made him jump forward with a jolt, he bellowed, "I do believe you are right! Let's move him now and see what happens," he said rushing back into the stable, thrusting on a headcollar and leading Mr Happy up the yard. "There's a box free in the top yard and he can go straight in there."

Mr Happy walked quietly beside him while Mr Butler patted his neck. "We'll get to the bottom of this Mr Happy, so that you can start living up to your name," he said.

The horses in the top yard whinnied as they heard the sound of approaching hooves. Mr Happy nickered back.

"Come and say hello to everyone," said Mr Butler as he led the horses to each of his new neighbours in turn. They snorted their welcomes. Their nostrils barely touching as they gently blew down their noses, their strange exchange of air a signal that they were friends.

Mr Happy walked around his new stable a few times pausing every now and again to sniff his thick bed of wood shavings. He slowly ate a few mouthfuls of hay, crunching it deliberately, did a few more circuits of his stable, and then stood with his head over the door. But now, instead of being pinned back, his ears were pricked forward, with the points nearly touching. Then he tossed his head and gave a shrill whinny. The others horses whinnied in return.

"If horses could smile, I am sure this chap would be beaming now," remarked Mr Butler.

Dixie leaned out of the kitchen window. "Well that's quite a different horse. Doesn't he look happy there? Good boy Mr Happy!"

"Thank young Tom here. It was his suggestion," said Mr Butler.

Tom felt so happy; he wanted to skip around the yard. "Well done Tom. That was a great observation, and because of you, Mr Happy is a happy horse," said Mr Heaven.

Emily gave Tom a spontaneous hug, and as he pulled away from her clutches, Ted punched his arm.

"I only said he doesn't like his neighbours," Tom said meekly.

"And you were the only one to spot it. I'm supposed to understand what makes these horses kick, but I missed this one!" laughed Mr Butler.

Chapter 11

After breakfast a few days later, Mrs Heaven announced, "Today's the day Chilli and Elvis come home from their holidays."

"I love Chilli and Elvis. They're so cute," Emily trilled.

"How can they be cute? They're horses," grumbled Ted.

"They are so quiet and kind and really gentle," Emily replied.

"They are super chaps, and it means I will be able to come on hacks with you guys. We'll be able to go further, which will do Tom's riding no end of good. And Dad will be able to ride at weekends too, when he's not on call," said Mrs Heaven.

"When are we getting them? This morning?" asked Tom.

"This afternoon Tom. We are seeing your mother this morning, so Emily and Ted are going to play with friends," said Mrs Heaven.

Tom's heart fell to the floor. He had forgotten about the meeting with his mother. His breathing came in short gasps as he tried to control the feelings that came surging to the surface. 'But I don't want to see her,' he thought to himself.

Emily and Ted took their cue from their mother and left the room. Mrs Heaven sat beside Tom.: "We've talked about this meeting many, many times and you will be fine. Jim and I will both be there with you and absolutely nothing can happen. Your social worker, Miss George, will be there too, and you won't for a moment be left alone with her."

Tom stared at the floor, his shoulders hunched, his hands on his knees. He fought the tears, telling himself over and over that nothing could go wrong. Mrs Heaven quietly put her arm around his shoulders, and he leant into her, the side of his face against her arm. But he couldn't stop the thoughts that scrambled through his mind as his past life and the fear associated with it came flooding back.

"Tom, your home is here now, with us. This is just helping your mum to accept that she will no longer be parenting you, and it is keeping the link open should you wish to have more access to see her more often," Mrs Heaven explained.

Tom sat, allowing himself to be hugged, while anxiety continued to rise in his chest. They heard the bang of the front door as Mr Heaven arrived home. Emily and Ted reappeared. "Group hug, everyone," said Mr Heaven sensing Tom needed as much love as they could all give him at that moment.

A short while later, with a heavy heart, Tom climbed into the car. He didn't know why, but he sensed everything was going to go wrong. First they drove to a pretty little house with a huge front garden. Ted and Emily jumped out of the car and rushed up the driveway to see their friends. Just before they went in to the house, they both turned and waved at Tom whose blank face stared out of the window. Tom said nothing on the journey to town. Eventually Mrs Heaven pulled up outside a bleak-looking building made of grey concrete.

It's gloomy appearance made Tom feel even more glum as they walked through the automatic doors to reception.

"I'll call Miss George," said the receptionist telling them to take a seat in the waiting area.

A few minutes later Miss George appeared. She was friendly and bustling, as usual, and talked through a few things with Tom. She told him that his mum was already waiting in the allocated room. She was with someone from the special hospital where she now lived. They would all be going into the room together. If she said anything that might distress Tom, the meeting would be terminated. She was in fine spirits and looking forward to seeing him. The stream of words kept coming from Miss

George but Tom wasn't taking any of it in. Finally she said, "Nothing bad can happen. I promise."

'Of course nothing bad can happen,' Tom told himself crossly wondering why he was so worried. Moments later he faced his mother. As soon as she saw him, she smiled warmly. It wasn't what he was expecting and he looked the other way, avoiding eye contact.

But then his mum seemed lost for words. "Er...Tom," she muttered, then nothing. She sat looking awkward, biting her lips, and sitting on her hands.

Tom glimpsed at her out of the corner of his eye and wondered how the monster of his dreams could look so helpless. He looked at Mr Heaven, and then Mrs Heaven in confusion and waited for his mum to speak, but instead an icy silence filled the room. He didn't know what she was thinking, and imagined it was how bad he was.

It was as if every time she tried to say something, she couldn't remember any words. Tom tried to speak, too. He wanted to speak, but the words refused to come out. It felt as if this went on like for an age. The person sat sitting with his mother put a reassuring arm around her, which seemed odd to Tom. After what she'd done how could anyone be nice to her? Then the tears started to tumble down her cheeks but she still remained silent. Now Tom almost felt sorry for his mother as she sat in her chair looking so sad, and he even ventured a glimmer of a smile. But she looked away, wiping the tears from her cheeks.

Eventually Miss George stood up and brought the meeting to a close. She led the way out of the room, with Tom close behind her, but he hesitated for a moment to look back at his mother. Mr and Mrs Heaven had already moved towards the door and suddenly Tom was alone. At that moment his mother grabbed his arm but he prised himself free and ran from the room, screaming. Panic overcame him, and his breathing increased rapidly leaving him gasping for air. He sunk to the floor and the tears surged upwards through his body. But he stifled them, saying to himself over and over again, 'I will not cry, I will not cry.'

Every part of his body trembled. He looked haunted, terrified.

Mr Heaven looked at his wife. She looked back. Both were thinking the visit had been a huge mistake. They knelt down either side of Tom, each taking one of his hands in one of theirs. But he didn't look at them. He didn't respond to their squeezes. He stared at the floor in front of him, his body shaking, his breaths still shallow and quick.

Mrs Heaven tried to sooth him. "Tom calm down. Nothing at all happened."

"Sh...-sh...-she... grabbed my arm," he sobbed.

"Yes, but that was all she did. She didn't hurt you. She just grabbed your arm."

"B...-b...-b...-but she wanted to take me away," Tom stuttered.

"No she didn't. I think she was just trying to reach out to you," said Mrs Heaven.

"She was going to take me back," Tom persisted in between his sobs.

"Tom you need to trust us on this. Nothing bad could have happened today. We were all there with you."

But Tom couldn't trust them. They had promised him nothing bad could happen, and it had. He knew that sooner or later she would be back to get him. Why hadn't he trusted his own feeling that today would go wrong? The love and safety he felt with the Heavens had gone. The only way he could cope was to create a barrier between himself and the rest of the world and that meant remaining silent.

Miss George beckoned to Mr and Mrs Heaven: "Take him home. He'll feel better soon. It's just all a bit raw for him."

"I feel as if this is all our fault. He was so brave about seeing his mother, even though he didn't really want to. We told him everything would be fine," Mrs Heaven said sadly.

"Let's take him home and let him spend some time with Leo.

That might help him to feel OK again," said Mr Heaven.

Tom was silent all the way home. At Hilltop House he hurried out of the car and rushed up to his bedroom, pushing the door shut behind him. Mrs Heaven knocked on the door and asked if he'd like to see Leo, but she was met with silence. Ted and Emily arrived home and the house immediately filled with laughter. But that quickly disappeared when they were told what had happened to Tom.

"Oh Mum, please let him be OK. He has to believe us that we all love him," said Emily sweetly.

"Shall I see if he wants to play on the computer?" asked Ted.

"You could try, but I don't think it would work," replied Mrs Heaven.

Tom refused to come down for lunch, so Mrs Heaven quietly put a plate of his favourite sandwiches in his room. The Heaven's chatted around the table during their meal, all hoping that Tom's beaming face would soon appear.

"Tom, we're going to fetch Elvis and Chilli now," Mrs Heaven called up the stairs.

Tom didn't respond.

"Jim, you stay here, in case he decides to come down and I'll take Emily and Ted with me to fetch the horses in from the meadow," sighed Mrs Heaven.

"Ted can lead Elvis, and I'll lead Chilli, although I'm sure they'd be absolutely fine if I led them both together," she said.

Upstairs, Tom heard them go. He wanted to see the big horses. He'd heard so much about Chilli and Elvis from Ted and Emily and had been looking forward to meeting them properly. But his fears were getting the better of him, and instead he decided he was going to run away and take Leo with him.

Later that night, Mr and Mrs Heaven crept into his room and kissed him lightly on the forehead, thinking he was fast asleep. He heard them go to bed and waited a few minutes until all the lights in the house were out, then crept down the stairs carrying a small rucksack filled with a jumper, his fluffy horse, his torch and a bottle of water. He wanted to take some biscuits from the cupboard, but he didn't want to steal from the Heavens again. Pulling on his wellingtons, a waterproof coat and a warm woolly hat, he crept outside, where a full moon lit up the landscape. In the distance he could see its bright white light glistening on the sea, while the surrounding sky was a deep inky blue. The wind was sharp and huge clouds laden with rain raced across the sky. Every now and again the moon was plunged into blackness as the clouds passed by, and then everything was bright again.

Tom crept up to the stable yard and called to Leo, who nickered in response. "Good boy, Leo. We're going away together, away from all this," he said.

He went into the tackroom, grabbed a bridle and fumbled with it for a while before eventually he managed to put it on Leo. Jumping on the pony's bare back, he rode up the driveway and then took the lane down to the beach.

'It's lucky there's such a huge moon and I can see,' he thought.

Leo walked steadily along the lane, the regular sound of his hoof beats helping to keep Tom's nerves at bay. But every time he heard a rustle in the hedge he shuddered, and every few moments he looked warily behind him, feeling sure he was being followed.

By the time they got to the beach, the wind was blowing quite fiercely and the waves were whipping themselves up into a fury. There was just enough beach to canter along to the mouth of the estuary, where the river met the sea. As the beach opened up to where they'd had the barbeque, Tom planned to take the coast path up over the cliffs, and find the small hut he'd often seen in the distance from Hilltop House. The tide seemed in a rush as it lapped backwards and forwards on the shore. Each time it came up the beach, it ate up a few more inches. Leo was jogged jogging along the shoreline narrow strip of sand when everything suddenly plunged into blackness as an enormous cloud crossed the moon and a huge downpour lashed down. Tom pulled his coat tightly around him. Leo thrust his ears back and started to jog sideways, desperately trying to put his hindquarters into the squall.

"Come on Leo, just a bit further," urged Tom kicking him on.

The water lapped up closer and closer to the shoreline, until eventually they were wading in it, and it grew deeper by the second. Tom shone his torch behind him. The waves were crashing against the cliffs. There was no way back.

He could see a bit more beach ahead of him, and Leo high-stepped through the water, sending spray upwards, as they reached the tiny piece of sand that remained. Leo's sides heaved as he regained his breath. Tom looked around him. They couldn't go forwards as there was no more beach. They couldn't go back they way they'd come as the waves were fiercely raging against the cliffs. Their tiny piece of sand was growing smaller and smaller and soon they would have to swim.

But Tom had never swum in his life. His heart pounded against his chest. He did not know what to do, and at the moment, he truly thought they would both die. Leo started pawing the ground and then set off into the sea.

"Leo, where are you going?" Tom sobbed, his voice getting lost on the wind. He wrapped his arms tightly around Leo's neck holding on with all his might.

Leo kept walking, going deeper and deeper into the water until eventually he started swimming back they way they had come. The tide was still rushing in and it helped push him up towards the slip road and safety, but he had to swim hard, to keep them away from the cliffs and certain death. On and on he paddled, at times his nostrils barely above the water. Every so often he slowed right down, exhausted, but Tom urged him on.

"Come on Leo. We can do this," he pleaded Tom, the wind snatching his words away. He kept patting the pony's neck and rubbing his mane, until his hands were so cold he could no longer feel them. He knew he couldn't hold on for much longer, and he felt Leo tiring underneath him. A wave hit them and he slipped from Leo back into the water. He felt sure he was going to go under, but suddenly he felt the sand beneath his feet. Finding strength from somewhere, he grabbed the reins and dragged Leo up the beach.

"Come on Leo. You can do this."

Leo was exhausted. Slowly he placed one foot in front of the other, dragging them through the sand, until Tom stopped pulling. They were under the cliffs where a natural overhang gave them some protection from the wind and rain. Slowly, Leo collapsed to his knees. The rest of his body followed and with a groan he sank to the floorground. He lay with his head and neck up, his nose resting on the sand. Tom huddled in close to him, shivering uncontrollably. His legs were soaking wet but his coat had somehow kept his body dry. Remembering the extra jumper he had in his rucksack, he managed to pull it on.

Leo let out another groan and than collapsed onto his side. Tom rubbed him earnestly, desperately trying to warm him up. "Leo, please don't die on me. I'm sorry," he said over and over again.

The moon appeared momentarily from behind a cloud, and Tom spotted an old tent someone must have left on the beach. He scrambled over and pulled it from the sand which half buried it. He covered Leo, weighing down the edges of the thin fabric with sand and then crept under it too, keeping his body as close to Leo's as he could in the hope that somehow they would warm each other up. Tom was so very cold, but the wind seemed less intense now. He pulled the tent tighter around himself, and started to feel a little bit warmer. He snuggled into Leo whose faint breathing was like a comforting pulse. He drifted off into a deep sleep, as the wind rustled the tent, and the waves crashed continuously against the rocks, rhythmic and constant.

Chapter 12

Mrs Heaven very slowly eased open Tom's door. She gasped. His bed was empty. Her heart gave a jolt and then she remembered that he was probably cuddled up with Leo in his stable. She called to her husband. "Jim, I'm just slipping up to the stables. Tom's bed is empty so he must be with Leo."

She rushed down the stairs, grabbed her coat and thrust her feet into her wellies. She pulled her coat tightly around her as the biting wind swirled through the air, grasping the leaves off the trees and sending them into a whirl. As she approached the stables, she had the feeling something was wrong. The ponies seemed restless and stood with their heads over their stables doors staring towards the sea in the distance. But Leo didn't appear. That's fine, Mrs Heaven comforted herself, he'll be lying in the straw with Tom. But Leo's stable door was slightly ajar. She rushed over and flung it wide open. The stable was empty. She ran to the tackroom and saw that Leo's bridle was missing from its peg. She rushed back to the house calling out to her husband. "Jim, he's taken Leo. They've been gone for most of the night. Leo's stable has barely been slept in."

Mr Heaven appeared with Emily and Ted.

"Where's he gone Mum?" shrieked Emily.

"We should call the police and report that he's missing," Mrs Heaven panicked.

"Let's just think this through," said Mr Heaven calmly. "Where would he go to hide from the world?"

His wife calmed down slightly and said: "I'll call Mr Butler and see if he's turned up there."

"You do that, Mandy while I have a quick scour around the fields to see if he's hiding under a hedge somewhere."

Mrs Heaven phoned the Butlers. Dixie answered, surprised at the early phone call. "Are you OK, Mandy?" she asked.

"No. It's Tom. He's gone missing with Leo. We wondered if he'd turned up there."

"We haven't seen him up here, but I'll go and check. The lads have been on the yard for an hour already and I'm sure they would have mentioned it. If he's not here, we'll come to yours to help you find him. But you need to think, Mandy, where does he feel happiest? Because that's where he'll be."

Mrs Heaven knew immediately: "He's happiest when he's with Leo, cantering I guess. That's when he feels free of all his troubles."

"Keep thinking about it. I'll let you know if he's turned up here," said Dixie, hanging up.

Mrs Heaven put the phone down absentmindedly, as she thought of all the places where Tom looked happy. In the school, practising his riding on Leo, in the field with Leo, in the stable with Leo and now they could add the racing stables to the list, the one place he was happy without Leo. Something was niggling Mrs Heaven. In the back of her mind she could hear Tom saying how he felt free. But she couldn't think where.

Emily crept over and tapped her gently. "Mum, what are we going to do? We need to find him. What if he's hurt, or sad on his own?"

"Sweetheart, we'll find him, I promise. We just need to think like he does, and imagine where he'd go if he felt sad."

"He'd go to the stable and lie with Leo. Or he'd gallop somewhere. Like on the beach. That's where he said he felt free. And he dreams about it too, he told me. Galloping along the beach with his arms outstretched like an aeroplane's wings."

"You're right Emily," exclaimed Mrs Heaven as she ran out of the house.

"Mum, where are you going?" shrieked Emily running after her.

"He's on the beach. That's where he's gone with Leo. Go and tell your Dad I'm going to drive down."

Mr Heaven appeared. "We're all coming love. We'll take the Land Rover. It's got all the kit in, just in case."

Mrs Heaven shuddered as another gust of wind blew across the hilltop, sending the fallen leaves swirling. Just as they started off, the Butlers' truck came thundering down the drive. Mr Butler wound down the window: "Any news?"

"Not yet. We're heading to the beach to see if he's gone there," replied Mr Heaven.

"Not much of a night to be on the beach. Those showers were fearsome, and there's a fair wind out at sea," said Mr Butler grimly.

Ben and Mickey sat perched on the edge of the seat in the back of the truck.

"We're here to help too, Mr Heaven," they called.

Mr Heaven only grunted his approval as he set off in the direction of the beach. They drove down the slip road to the edge of the sand and could see the waves pounding against the cliffs. The tide was still high, and there was barely any beach.

The two vehicles parked up. Peering down the slip road, Mr Heaven said: "We'll have to walk along the cliff path to the beach at the end. Let's hope he's found shelter there." He zipped his coat up to his chin and pulled his hood over his head.

He pulled his medical kit out of the Land Rover and put two foil survival blankets into his pocket.

The Heavens made their way up the roughly hewn steps to the cliff carpark high above the beach and started walking along the path. The Butlers and Mickey followed.

"I'll just take a scout down on the beach at this end," called Ben.

"Not much point in that. There's nowhere for them to shelter," shouted Mr Butler above the wind.

"I'll take a look anyway. There's a bit of beach behind those rocks," said Ben.

"You're wasting your time," grumbled Mr Butler.

Ben sprinted off down the slip road and stood at the edge of the water. Mr Butler was right, he thought, there really wasn't enough beach to take shelter. He was just about to leave when he noticed a sliver of sand disappearing behind a huge rocky outcrop that jutted into the sea. There was barely enough exposed sand to avoid his feet getting wet, but he crept gingerly along it until the area widened out to reveal a small sheltered beach cocooned on three sides by the cliffs and rocks.

Ben saw the old tent. Puzzled, he took a closer look, thinking it odd that it had been laid out in the way it had, its edges covered with sand to stop it blowing away. Tentatively, he pulled back one corner and was shocked and relieved at the same time by what he saw. Tom lay huddled in a ball against Leo's outstretched neck. He looked like he was in a deep sleep, but at least he was breathing. Leo was quite still. Ben felt for a pulse under the pony's cheekbone and felt a glimmer of a beat. 'Well that has to be a good thing,' he thought to himself as he took off his coat, and wrapped it around Tom. Then he yelled to the others on the cliff path above: "I've found them! They're both here, and alive."

There was a commotion as everyone appeared around the sandy bluff, which was getting wider by the minute as the tide began to go out. They all ran over to the stricken pony and Tom.

"Hush now," said Mr Heaven kneeling down. "We need peace and quiet here."

"I took Leo's pulse and it's there, just, but I didn't want to touch him, although believe me, I was sorely tempted to rub some life into him."

"Good work Ben," Mr Heaven said.

Tom started to come to, and drowsily asked where he was.

"Everything is just fine, Tom. You're safe with us now," said Mr Heaven.

Mrs Heaven asked him to stand up and move around to warm up. She wrapped a blanket around him.

Tom's eyes widened as everything came flooding back to him. He felt so relieved to see everyone. 'They came to find me. They must like me,' he thought. And then he remembered Leo. "Leo, where's Leo. You have to save Leo," he whimpered.

"Leo's here Tom. Right beside you. He's still alive, but we need to know what happened."

Tom couldn't speak.

"I...we..." he stuttered.

"It's alright love, just take your time," said Mrs Heaven gently.

Tom took several gulps and tried again: "We...the...water, sea. It came in fast. And we were stuck. So he swam, and saved us. Then he fell over. Here."

"The chances are he's exhausted. Let's just see if we can warm him up a little," said Mr Heaven taking the two survival blankets and wrapping them around the pony. He asked Mr Butler to go back to his truck and get some water.

"If he comes around, he'll be wanting a drink, and I'll pop something in the water that will help him too."

"Is he going to be OK?" asked Tom in a whisper and then shouted: "Look, he blinked his eyes."

They all glanced over and sure enough, Leo's eyes were open. Then with a huge snort, he heaved his head and neck off the ground and lay there, resting the tip of his nose on the sand. Tom tried to scramble towards him, but Ben grabbed him and held him tight.

"Leave him be for a minute. He needs a little space to get his bearings."

Tom nodded, but his eyes were wide with fear. This was the worst moment in his life, he thought. Worse than when his mother locked him in the cupboard.

Mr Butler arrived with half a bucket of water. Mr Heaven offered it to Leo and the pony took a few sips. "Just a bit at a time lad. Don't gulp, otherwise that will make you even more poorly," Mr Heaven said, taking the bucket away.

Mrs Heaven knelt down beside Tom. "He's going to be just fine," she reassured him.

"But what if he dies? It will be my fault," he said sniffing back the tears.

Mr Heaven offered Leo some more water and he took a few more sips. His ears started to twitch and then, with a huge groan, he lurched to his feet. He peered around him, and snorted at the survival blankets, which had slipped to the ground. Tom pulled away from Mrs Heaven and, rushing over, flung his arms around Leo's neck. Leo nickered and then nuzzled him, searching for a treat.

"I think he's going to be OK Tom. Let's just give him a bit more water," said Mr Heaven offering him the bucket again. Leo drank readily this time and then impatiently started to paw the ground.

"Mandy, could you slip back home and get the horsebox? It's a long walk back up the hill and I think we'll need to wrap him in cotton wool for a bit," said Mr Heaven.

Mrs Heaven scooted off to the Land Rover.

After she'd gone, Mr Heaven swopped Leo's stiff waterlogged bridle for a dry headcollar and lead rope. He ran his hands down each of the pony's legs to check for cuts or swelling. Once he had satisfied himself that there was nothing too much to worry about, he said: "Ben would you just lead him away from me please, and then walk back. We need to see if he's lame from his swim."

"Certainly Mr Heaven," replied Ben taking the lead rope and walking slowly away.

Leo took one tentative step after the other, as if he was testing whether his legs still worked.

“He’s certainly very stiff, and if he was a human you’d stick him straight in a warm bath. But he’ll live to tell the tale. A good long rest, a bit of pain relief and he’ll be just fine,” said Mr Heaven.

“Do you hear that Tom?” Ben was so excited he gave Tom an almighty shove, which sent the boy flying into the sand. “Oh sorry lad, forgot my strength there, and that you’re as light as a feather. Not that that is a bad thing, with the pony racing and stuff,” he gabbled.

“It’s fine,” said Tom hauling himself up. He noticed everyone was staring at him and stared into the ground, wishing it would swallow him up. He desperately wanted to say sorry. He wanted to tell them that he would never let them down again. But the words wouldn’t come out. Instead, he shuffled from one foot to the other.

Mr Heaven knelt down so that his eyes were level with Tom’s. “Tom,” he said seriously, “you have to trust us. You have a choice. Either you accept that we want you to live as part of our family, or you decide it’s not what you want. It’s your choice.”

Tom nodded meekly. A huge tear dropped to the ground. “I’m…sorry.”

Mr Heaven hugged him. “Come on, let’s see if Mandy is here with the horsebox and get Leo back home for some food and a lie down.”

Chapter 13

For that day and most of the rest of the next, Tom felt exhausted and slept in his bed snuggled up in a warm fleecy blanket. Eventually Mrs Heaven came upstairs and, after knocking gently on the door, came in and sat down on his bed. She asked him what had caused him to run away. He'd thought about it a lot, and was ready for the question: "When she grabbed my arm, Mum I mean, I thought she was snatching me back. I don't want to go back, ever. I want to stay here."

Mrs Heaven sighed. "You know Tom, it's a shame that your mum was unable to speak to you. I think if she had you wouldn't have run away."

"What do you mean?" he shrugged.

"After we left, Miss George spoke with her for a long time. She grabbed you because she wanted to hug you. She didn't know how to tell you how sorry she is, for everything, and in desperation she grabbed your arm. And it frightened you. She knows what she did is wrong. She also understands that she is a very sick person, and that she can no longer look after you."

"Thank goodness for that," mumbled Tom before saying: "It doesn't matter that she's ill, or whatever else it is, I won't ever go back with her, ever."

"And you don't have to go back there, ever," said Mrs Heaven. "Which leads me on to another little matter."

Tom gulped, thinking he was about to hear some bad news.

"While you've been sleeping, you've become a member of the

local Pony Club, so that you can go to a training day for pony racing, and a couple of rallies too."

Tom's eyes lit up. "So you'll still let me ride Leo and go racing?"

"Why wouldn't we?" asked Mrs Heaven.

"Well...you know...because I took him, and he nearly drowned."

"Hush now Tom. Put that behind you. We all do things we shouldn't. The secret is to learn from our mistakes."

"I dunno what I'm s'posed to have learnt, but I know one thing. I'm not running away again. Well not until I've learned to swim anyway," said Tom seriously.

Mrs Heaven laughed. "Well before you learn to swim, we need to get a bit more riding practice in if we're to get you riding on a racecourse this autumn."

"Can we go riding now? I feel much better."

"Not now, but in a couple of days time. We want to make sure Leo is well and truly over his adventure before he starts pony race training. But you can come up to the yard and meet Elvis and Chilli properly if you like," said Mrs Heaven.

Tom leapt out of his bed. "Yes please," he said, rushing around putting on his clothes.

Mrs Heaven was so relieved that Tom seemed to have found his zest again she didn't know whether to laugh or cry. Instead, she called loudly, "Ted, Emily! We're all going up to the yard together."

The children appeared in an instant, as if they'd been waiting for this moment. Emily rushed over to Tom and flung her arms around him. As he unwrapped himself from her hug, Ted held up his hand for a high five.

"Does this mean you'll be riding with us, with Skip and Henry and Elvis and Chilli and Ted and Mum, altogether, like a cavalcade?" asked Emily.

"Well, yes, I guess," said Tom looking at Mrs Heaven questioningly.

"Of course it does. Nothing has changed at all. Back to normal.

Except, no riding backwards," she said sternly.

The children giggled as they rushed down the stars like a pack of over-excited puppies.

Tom hadn't seen Leo since their adventure and when the pony heard him coming up the path towards the stables he kicked his door eagerly and tossed his head.

"We'll have none of that kicking of doors Leo," called Mrs Heaven.

Chilli and Elvis put their heads out of their stables and stared inquisitively at the rabble approaching them. Chilli was a bright bay with a black mane and tail and a curious white cross in the centre of his face. He was very tall and gangly with a high wither and a long neck. He looked questioningly at Tom, wondering who this small skinny boy was, and when Tom offered his hand, he sniffed it gently, barely touching it with the fine hair on his nostrils, before staring away into the distance, his huge brown eyes wide with wonder.

Mrs Heaven put a headcollar on him and tied him outside his stable. Emily fussed around him and he loved all the attention. He was so tall Tom barely came above his elbow. But he looked very wise and was careful not to step on Tom, while Mrs Heaven and Emily groomed him, although his coat twitched every now and again as they touched a ticklish spot.

"This horse is a wonderful old boy. He's won us so many point-to-points. We've had a lot of fun with him," said Mrs Heaven fondly.

"How old is he?"

"He's ten now," said Mrs Heaven.

"That doesn't sound very old."

"It isn't really," agreed Mrs Heaven. "He's a real gentleman, and gives everyone such a safe ride we let the younger jockeys ride him in novice rider races."

"Can I ride him over the big fences at Mr Butler's one day?" Tom asked eagerly.

Mrs Heaven laughed. "One day Tom, but you need to master the show jumps in the school first, and then we'll go hunter trialling."

Ted started to help groom Chilli too and it was clear to Tom that the family adored him. When he was polished and gleaming, they rugged him up in a smart blue quilted rug and then gave Elvis the same grooming treatment.

Elvis was jet black and smaller than Chilli. He had a thick neck and looked like a powerhouse of energy. Tom thought he was the most beautiful horse he'd ever seen, even more beautiful than Francome when he'd jumped over the big fences. His black coat shone and his mane and tail fell in soft waves. His nose was slightly dished, which made him look very pretty, and he had enormous eyes and long eye lashes. Tom walked around him in awe while Elvis cocked an ear back, watching every move out of the corner of his eye.

"You need to be a little more careful of Elvis. Don't stand behind him, as when he's feeling impatient, he'll kick out," warned Mrs Heaven.

Only half listening, Tom walked up to Elvis's head and in utter admiration started stroking down his neck. Elvis bent his head around and nuzzled Tom in the side. Leo whinnied.

"Sorry Leo," called Tom, hurrying over to the pony with a grooming kit. "Just a couple more days and I'll be able to ride you again."

"There's something else I need to talk to you about," Mrs Heaven called.

Ted and Emily both yelled in unison: "School!"

Tom raised his eyes heavenwards.

"Oh that," he said.

"Well yes, next week you'll be going to the local primary school with Emily. The same school I teach part time at so I'll be able to keep an eye on you."

Tom wasn't bothered about going back to school. He enjoyed

learning and had never had any trouble at school. He was more anxious about being ready for the training day. "So when will I be able to practise?" he asked.

Mrs Heaven was relieved that he taken the prospect of returning to school in his stride. "We can ride when you get home as the school's got floodlights, unless the weather is bad, and then we won't bother. But really Tom, how do you feel about going back to school?" she asked again, just to be sure.

"Oh fine. I quite like it," he shrugged, his mind fixed on when he'd be riding again.

"Mandy," he called. "How good is my cantering?"

"It's good, and its probably improved since your little trip down to the beach bareback."

Tom groaned. "Do we have to talk about that again?"

"No we don't, but you brought it up, in a roundabout way!"

Tom went back to fussing over Leo, taking off his rugs and giving him a thorough groom. Then, when he thought no one was looking, he swung up onto the pony's back, and bent his legs, jockey style. Leaning down he whispered to Leo, "Just so you get used to me riding with my stirrups short," and then leapt back into the straw when he heard Mandy approaching.

"Tom, there's someone here you might like to meet," she called.

He groaned. All he wanted to do was mess around with the horses and ponies, safe in his dream world.

"Doubt it," he called back. "I've met everyone I've ever wanted to meet," and he started reeling off names: "Mr Butler, Dixie, Ben and Mickey."

"But I know you'll like her," Mrs Heaven persisted.

"Why would I like her?" he asked peering over the door.

"Oh come on. I promise you'll like her. What if I told you she is a jockey?"

Tom rushed out the door, took a few strides across to the other side of the yard and stood next to Elvis who nuzzled his hair expectantly.

"Meet Hannah, Tom. She's going to ride out either Elvis or Chilli during the winter and will be riding Chilli in novice rider races in point-to-points."

Suddenly feeling very shy, Tom fixed his eyes to the ground and muttered hello.

"Cat got your tongue?" asked Hannah laughing. She had a loud, husky voice, and oozed confidence as she slapped Elvis on the neck, making him jump.

"He doesn't like being whacked on the neck like that. No horse does. Scratch him on his neck," said Tom, defiance streaked across his face. He took an instant dislike to her and he couldn't explain why.

"Well now, for such a wee lad, you're not afraid of saying what you think," Hannah said, reaching her arm up to the top of Elvis's mane. Elvis went into a trance as Hannah scratched away.

"Told you," said Tom.

"That you did," replied Hannah.

I'll keep an eye on that one, thought Tom as he returned to Leo's stable.

Emily followed him: "Why didn't you stay and talk to Hannah? We thought you'd like it that she goes around riding peoples racehorses for them."

"I dunno, I just don't like her," he said grumpily.

"Well you need to like her, as she'll be here every morning," Emily said.

"No I won't. She's loud and gruff and she frightens the horses," replied Tom.

"She does not."

"She does. You'll see," he said and then ignored her as he brushed out Leo's tail.

He heard Hannah call to Mrs Heaven that she'd see her on Monday morning, before driving away fast up the lane.

"Well Tom, you surprised me there. We all thought you'd

like to meet a teenager who rides out horses for lots of different trainers," remarked Mrs Heaven.

"Well I don't. She's too rough. You don't need to be slappy happy around horses. They prefer calm and quiet," said Tom.

"I'm not quite sure how you've worked all of that out in the five minutes you've seen her, but you are probably right. She's just ambitious and wants to impress. But I'm sure we can teach her she can get there by being kind," said Mrs Heaven.

Chapter 14

"Everyone ready?" called Mr Heaven as he entered the kitchen. He wore an old pair of navy blue breeches, a black skullcap with no cover, which made him look like he was wearing a bowl, and an ancient pair of brown jodphur boots. It was the weekend and the first time the family were riding all together. Tom and the children had been looking forward to it for ages.

"Dad, what are you wearing? It's not a fancy dress party," laughed Ted gawping at his father's baggy breeches.

"Once a stable lad, always a stable lad," his father laughed. "This attire is similar to what we all wore when we rode out at the local racing yards. Shall we go then?"

The children skipped ahead to the stables.

"So where are we going today? Around the lanes, or for a canter in the woods?" he called after them.

"Canter in the woods," they shrieked in unison.

"Calm down. We're only going for a hack, not a gallop around Cheltenham racecourse," he laughed.

Leo felt the excitement in the air and started to pace his stable expectantly. Every so often he peered over his door, before walking another circuit of the loose box.

Grabbing his headcollar, Tom walked over to him, talking quietly. "Easy now Leo," he said, opening the stable door. He quickly put on the headcollar and tied the pony up. Deftly, he removed Leo's rugs and gave him a brush over before tacking him up.

He was about to lead Leo out of his stable and get on, when he saw that Emily was only just coming out of the tackroom carrying Skip's tack.

"What's taking you so long?" Tom called.

"Well I had to plait my hair, and then I had to go back to the house and get Skip's pink saddle pad, and then my coat didn't match, so I went back to get a different one..."

"Hand it here," said Tom interrupting her and grabbing the saddle and bridle.

"Oh thanks, Tom. I've always wanted my own slave," she laughed.

"I'm not your slave, I just want to get going," he groaned.

Five minutes later Skip was ready and before long the family set off with Chilli leading the way, the children in between and Elvis bringing up the rear with Mrs Heaven on board.

Tom quietly smoothed Leo's neck as he was growing quite excited being in a group. "You're alright boy. Nothing can happen to you," he said soothingly, letting his reins go long so that the pony felt no pressure on his mouth. Leo understood. He cocked an ear back, stopped jogging and walked quietly beside Henry.

Skip grabbed a mouthful of leaves from the hedge. "Emily, don't let him do that. It's bad manners," called Mrs Heaven.

"But he's hungry," her daughter replied.

"No he's not. He's taking advantage of you being too busy chatting to notice," said her mother.

"Skip, Mum says you're not to do that," said Emily, doing nothing at all to stop him.

Tom trotted to the front to ride beside Mr Heaven who had his stirrups a little shorter than you'd normally expect on a hack.

"You look like a jockey up there," laughed Tom looking at Mr Heaven who seemed to tower above him. Chilli was so tall with an enormous neck that stretched out in front of him, huge loppy ears and such a big stride that Leo had to jog to keep up. As he walked along, the big horse almost seemed to be smiling and turned his head to peer at Leo and Tom beside him giving them a look of encouragement.

"Once you've ridden short, you always ride short. Feels safer somehow," Mr Heaven said.

Tom thought about it for a minute: "Did you used to be a jockey too?"

"I was once, a long time ago, and a very bad one at that. I only rode in point-to-points but had a few rotten falls, so decided the life of a jockey wasn't for me and concentrated on being a vet."

"You never told me that," Tom said amazed that Mr Heaven had kept this wonderful fact a secret.

"It's not that I didn't tell you on purpose, I just didn't think it was worth telling."

"So why did you keep falling off?" asked Tom.

"I fell off because I never learned to slip my reins, and would hang on for dear life, and then come off over the shoulder when the horse landed after the fence," replied Mr Heaven. He reflected for a short while and then added, "I am also very tall and bulky too. Not the perfect shape for a jockey. Sometimes the horses I rode were quite slight and I felt like I was riding a pony. Unlike you Tom. You are small and light, with plenty of strength. You're agile as well and a brilliant rider, which to my mind are the perfect attributes for any jockey."

Tom blushed at the compliment. He knew he felt very at home on a pony but he wouldn't go so far as to say he was brilliant. Still, it did make him feel very happy, as he patted Leo and told him he was a good boy.

"Did you like being a jockey?" Tom asked.

"I loved it. You make some real friends in the changing room and it's always a laugh," Mr Heaven said wistfully.

Tom thought for a few moments: "What is it really like, sailing of those fences and galloping really fast?"

"There is no better feeling in the world. The adrenalin rush you get is like nothing else. It's a wonderful thing to do. You feel the power of the horse underneath you and when they jump a fence...well it is the most astounding feeling. Quite breathtaking. Better than the biggest big dipper at the fairground or the most terrifying funfair ride."

"I don't know what either of those are like," mumbled Tom.

"You'll get a far better buzz jumping and riding than anything like that can give you. It's you and your horse, together as one, taking on the world, so to speak."

Tom thought Mr Heaven was starting to talk gobbledegook and put it down to the fact that being on Chilli was transporting him back to that special world.

"So it was brilliant even though you got hurt and stuff?"

"If you're worrying about getting hurt, then it's not something you should ever think of doing. Every race you enter, you have to go in thinking you can win, not of the possibilities of a fall. If you're positive, your horse will feel it," said Mr Heaven.

"But what about when you're hurt?" pressed Tom.

"Oh that! Well to be honest, you don't feel it when it happens. And your bones soon mend. The thrill of riding far and away outweighs the thought of getting hurt."

"So why did you really give up Mr Heaven?" pushed Tom.

Mr Heaven glanced at Tom grinning: "Ahh you've caught me out. Do you really want to know?"

"Yes," said Tom nodding eagerly.

"OK, but you are never ever to use the information I am about to give you against me. Never, not now or in the future."

Tom gulped, wondering what on earth it could be that stopped Mr Heaven from riding in races.

"I-got-too--fat." Mr Heaven blurted out.

Tom yowled in laughter. The way Mr Heaven had spluttered the words was so comical. He clutched his tummy trying hard to stop the laughter erupting from his body.

Emily trotted up beside him. "What's wrong Tom? What's

wrong with Tom, Dad? Why is he crying? He looks like he's in pain."

She sounded so worried Tom tried to say that he was fine. But his words came out in gasps and Emily grew more panic-stricken than ever.

She screeched: "Dad help him. He's going to explode or something."

She looked up to her father on Chilli and saw that he was trying hard not to laugh.

"Why are you laughing at Tom being so ill? Dad stop it," she yelled.

"Emily he's laughing. He's fine. But he can't stop."

By this time, Tom was bent double over Leo's neck, one arm around his stomach, the other clutching the reins. Every time he tried to stop laughing, he spluttered the word "fat" again and then collapsed into further reels of laughter.

"Dad what's he on about?" Emily looked back at Ted who was in a world of his own, gazing over the hedgerows, and then noticed her mum was giggling too. "Mum, what's going on? Why is Tom behaving like that?" she said.

"It's up to your father to tell you, if my guess is right," she laughed.

"Dad, tell me now. It's not fair if you tell Tom things and not me," she demanded.

Mr Heaven realised he had to tell his daughter the truth, otherwise something ominous could creep into their family life – the last thing the Heavens needed was their children to start feeling jealous of Tom. Sometimes he thought Emily was a bit put out at having Tom around, but he tried to put it out of his mind.

"Emily, much as it saddens me to have to do it, as I fear you will catch the same condition as Tom, I will tell you," he said very seriously. "Ted, I need you to listen to my confession."

"What? Are you talking to me?" Ted said.

"Yes Ted I am. Now, listen up. As you are both aware, until a few years ago, I used to ride in point-to-points. I have always said that I gave up because I kept falling off. This is only part of the truth..."

At that moment, Chilli spooked as a falling leaf dropped on his nose. He snorted, his hooves clattered on the tarmac. Leo jumped too, and like a deck of falling cards, all five horses had their moment, creating a crescendo of sound on the road before settling back down again.

"The sound of their hooves frightens me more than the actual spook," said Emily patting Skip.

"You're right there," called Mrs Heaven. "The horses barely move, but the crashing of their hooves really wakes you up."

The jolt brought Tom out of his hysterical laughing and, quite relieved, he sat up, took a hold of both reins and rode normally again. Mr Heaven breathed a sigh of relief, thinking he'd got away with not telling his children the truth and silently thanked Chilli and the leaf.

Then Emily piped up, "Go on, Dad."

Mr Heaven sighed: "The reason I gave up riding in races is because I ate too much and got very fat!"

"Is that it?" said Emily incredulously. "You're very, very tall Dad, so it's brilliant that you rode in races." Not for the first time, his young daughter surprised him with her practical outlook on life. Ted agreed, wondering to himself what all the fuss was about.

Mr Heaven winked at Tom, who grinned back, then he put up his arm, bringing everyone to a halt, and turning in the saddle he said, "We are just about to go into the woods. I need you to listen as we don't want any out-of-control ponies. In a minute or two the path widens and at that point we can up the speed. I will lead at a steady canter, then Tom, followed by Emily, then Ted with Mum bringing up the rear.

"Keep it steady, and if any of you get into any difficulties, just shout."

"I think the only one who may get into trouble is me. Elvis is feeling very fresh today," laughed Mrs Heaven.

Chilli jumped off at a steady canter when he was asked to by Mr Heaven. It was if he knew he was babysitting young riders. He didn't try and go faster, and just maintained a steady, rhythmic pace, de-dum, de-dum.

Leo snatched at the bit, eager to go faster. Tom bridged his reins as Mrs Heaven had shown him in the school. "Steady boy," he said, feeling comfortable, even though Leo clearly had ideas of overtaking Chilli. His arms soon ached, but he kept his hands very still, and instead of yanking the reins, he shifted his weight very slightly in the saddle so that his body formed a pivot against the pulling pony. Leo started to relax, and began to canter more calmly.

"You're not going anywhere. There's no rush. Just relax." Tom talked constantly to the pony who flicked an ear back as he listened.

Mr Heaven glanced behind, taking in everything that Tom was doing while Mrs Heaven, from her place at the back of the string, did the same. All too soon they slowed to a trot and then drew to a walk.

"Everyone OK?" called Mr Heaven.

"That was brilliant. Skip loved that," Emily said excitedly.

Ted was grinning. "I think that's as fast as Henry can go," he laughed.

"Do you want to jump a few logs, Ted?" asked Mr Heaven.

Ted's face lit up. "Yes please."

"Can I?" asked Tom.

"Not today. And not for any other reason than you did very well with Leo just then. He's relaxed now and we don't want him getting excited," said Mrs Heaven.

Tom was desperate to jump, but he knew Leo's education was more important if they were to be able to take part in pony races.

Mr Heaven veered off down another wide woodland track.

Along one side was a row of log piles. "We'll trot along the path and you jump the jumps," he said.

As Ted rode Henry towards the jumps, he set off beside him on Chilli. The pair cleared every one neatly with Mr Heaven keeping pace.

"Skip would never to do that," said Emily, rather relieved that her pony didn't like jumping.

"Why don't you have a go Dad?" asked Ted.

"Oh I don't know. It's been many years since I jumped."

"Go on Dad. You can do it. And if you fall off again, we're all here to catch you," Emily said.

Mr Heaven trotted Chilli back up to the end of the line of log piles, turned and set off at a canter along the leaf-strewn track. As if realising he had a very rusty rider on his back, Chilli jumped very slowly and deliberately. Mr Heaven didn't really have to do anything, except sit there, which he was quite happy to do.

"That was just brilliant," he said, puffing a little as he pulled up. "Maybe I'll school over those big fences up at the Butler's one day," he joked. Chilli stood quite still as Mr Heaven fussed him, thinking to himself that he would never have been brave enough to jump if he hadn't been sat on this wonderful horse.

They turned for home, winding their way back through the woods along the soft earthy tracks. It was a perfect autumn day. No one spoke as they listened to their horses' gentle hoof beats and the noise of birdsong. Every now and again they snapped twigs sending pheasants squawking and birds twittering to a new roost in the branches.

Chapter 15

The horses were tucked up in their stables with full nets of hay and the children sat around the kitchen table. It was nearly dark outside and the rain spattered against the window as the wind howled around the house. A stormy night was forecast. Gazing out to sea, Tom shuddered.

Mrs Heaven drew shut all the curtains, blocking out the gloomy night. The yellow material was dashed with bright red poppies and it was as if sunshine had poured into the room. She placed a piping hot dish of lasagne on the table and everyone dived in. They were hungry, tired and ruddy cheeked after their long ride and they piled their plates high. Mr Heaven hobbled over to join them. His legs were slightly apart and bent at the knees and it looked as though he was still astride a horse.

"What's up with you cowboy?" joked Mrs Heaven.

"These poor stiff legs of mine are protesting about the three-hour hack having not been on a horse for more than six months," he said grimacing as he sat at the table.

Mrs Heaven joined them. The conversation lulled as everyone ate hungrily.

"Next weekend there's a Pony Club racing rally at Mr Butler's. After today's ride, we think Tom is ready to go," said Mrs Heaven.

Tom stopped eating. "On Leo?" he asked.

"Yes on Leo!"

"Are we going too?" asked Emily sounding quite tetchy.

Sometimes it seemed to her that Tom was the only person that mattered around here.

"Not next weekend Emily. Tom loves the idea of racing so much we thought it would be a great opportunity for him to stay with the Butlers and have a chance to experience the whole world of racing and racehorses."

Tom's eyes widened. At first he thought he had misheard Mrs Heaven until she said, "Are you OK with that Tom, staying with the Butlers?"

He nodded eagerly.

"It's not fair. Why's Tom going and not us?" Emily whined.

"Why would you want to spend a whole weekend riding?" said Ted and Emily kicked him under the table.

"Well I wouldn't," he said. "Anything's better than all day and every day with horses." Ted was hungry, and when he was hungry, nothing was more important than eating so he really wasn't bothered what happened the following weekend.

Tom stared at his food feeling awkward. He always noticed things, and he'd noticed Emily wasn't entirely happy with him living at Hilltop House. Now she wasn't happy about him going to the Butlers. He couldn't win.

"While Tom has a little tuition about race riding we are all going on a special weekend away," said Mrs Heaven.

Emily gasped. "You mean we're going on a mini holiday without Tom?" she said excitedly. She glanced at Tom feeling a tiny bit guilty but she didn't really care. A weekend with just her mum, dad and brother was the best news she'd had in ages.

Tom didn't take any notice. The thought of spending the weekend with Mr Butler and Dixie was so exciting he could hardly contain himself.

Mr and Mrs Heaven sighed with relief.

"Where are we going?" badgered Emily.

"We are going to London to see some sights," said Mrs Heaven.

"Who's looking after the horses?" asked Tom.

"You're taking Leo with you to the Butlers, and Hannah will look after the others. So it's all sorted."

Tom frowned. He just didn't trust Hannah. He got a horrible feeling in the pit of his stomach when he even just thought about her.

The following Friday straight after school, Mrs Heaven packed the final bits and pieces that Tom and Leo might need. As she fussed with all the kit, Tom pulled his saddle from the back of the Land Rover and sneaked it back into the tackroom making sure no one had seen him.

At last they were ready to leave.

"I think we've packed everything but the kitchen sink," laughed Mrs Heaven as she climbed into the driver's seat.

Emily and Ted appeared with Mr Heaven who was over the top in his farewells, making Tom flinch with his man hugs and back slaps. "You'll have a wonderful time," he said loudly, as if somehow the volume of his voice equated to how much the family would miss him.

Mrs Heaven laughed. "Jim. He's going away for two nights. You don't need to over-egg it quite so much!"

"Look, I really, really, really am looking forward to going to the Butlers. I can't wait to ride Leo up the gallops," Tom said.

Emily shuffled over. "Um. I'll miss you Tom," she said half-heartedly.

"Yeah, yeah, I know you want me to stay really. I can if you like," said Tom winking at her mischievously. Then he blurted out, "Ems, I know what you're thinking. And I don't mind. You need to spend time with your mum and dad without me around. And I don't want you to think I'd get in your way. Anything here is better than how it used to be. You're all great for being so kind to me." It was the most he'd ever said about his life to anyone.

"Oh," said Emily quite taken aback. She didn't know what to say, but she felt very relieved by his words. She gave him a shy hug.

"Time to go," called Mrs Heaven. Tom settled himself into the passenger seat and they set off.

She navigated confidently around the twisting lanes flanked on either side by high Devon banks, which made it feel like they were driving along roofless tunnels. Within a short time they arrived at the entrance to Hall Farm Racing Stables and swept along the driveway past the post-and-railed paddocks to the house where Mrs Heaven took a left fork in the driveway that led down to the stable yard. Dixie appeared from a stable and swooping over to Tom lifted him up and gave him the most enormous hug.

"Come on, let's get Leo settled with the children's ponies," she said.

They opened up the front ramp of the trailer and Tom led him off. He stood and gazed for a few moments taking in his new surroundings before carefully walking down the ramp. His new stable was filled with a thick bed of straw and there was a full haynet waiting.

As they unpacked the tack, Tom wailed, "Uh oh. I've forgotten the saddle."

Mrs Heaven looked perplexed: "How can that be? I distinctly remember packing it."

"Oh don't worry," said Dixie. We'll nip over in the morning, when Hannah's there so that we can be sure the tackroom is unlocked."

"Are you sure?" said Mrs Heaven. "It would save me a lot of bother and we can get off up to London when I get back."

"Of course I am sure. Tom can't ride Leo until all the racehorses have been exercised so we'll have plenty of time, and then Ben's going to take him up on the gallops before the rally on Sunday."

"Oh you are an angel," said Mrs Heaven hugging her friend and then doing the same to Tom. Kneeling down in front of him, she placed her hands on his arms and said, "Tom, we'll really miss you this weekend, and you know we all love you very much."

"I do know that, Mandy. I can tell Emily's not that happy about having me around at the moment, but tell her I'll make sure Skip is fine." Mandy nodded calmly. She knew by now that Tom didn't miss much that went on around him, but she could also see that he'd come a long way in the last few weeks and was no longer worried that they would send him away.

After they waved goodbye, Dixie led him back to the house to meet her children: Charlie, who was the same age as him, Henry, her oldest son, who was 14, and Amelia who was 16. They didn't really seem interested in Tom, and he wasn't very interested in them, so he sat quietly watching the telly.

Mr Butler was busy in his office. He appeared just before five o'clock with his thick grey hair ruffled so that it stood on end, his shirt half untucked and a general look of untidiness about him. "One of those days. Paper work," he said to Tom by way of an apology for his disheveled appearance, and invited him to accompany him at evening stables. "It's when I go to every horse's box, check their legs and other signs that they are feeling one hundred per cent. It'll take an hour or so but it's part and parcel of the job, and the part of the parcel I love," he joked.

Tom nodded eagerly and they set off to the stable yard. Mr Butler checked each horse, going from stable to stable. He ran his hands down both their front legs looking for any signs of injury and chatted to the lads who looked after them. Tom followed closely behind him taking everything in.

"So what does that do?" he asked after Mr Butler had checked about fifty horses.

"I wondered when you'd find your tongue. By feeling the legs I can detect signs of heat. If there is heat, it means the horse might be suffering an injury and we should take action."

Tom nodded in wonder and decided he'd start feeling Leo's legs every day, just in case. That night he went to bed as happy as he had ever been, snuggled up with his fluffy horse. The house creaked and sighed through the darkness, and Tom tossed and turned. He was barely able to sleep in these strange surroundings but he wasn't worried, so he lay there thinking about all the wonderful horses he had met that day until he drifted off to sleep.

Next morning the dawn had yet to creep into the sky, but Tom was wide awake and he decided to get up. He dressed quickly and dashed downstairs. Dixie was in the kitchen making a huge pot of tea. She told him Mr Butler had already left the house to oversee the feeding of the horses. "He'll be back at ten, after the first lot, for breakfast."

"Can I go and see to Leo?" he asked.

"Of course you can love. Ask Sarah to help you find the things you need. She looks after the kids' three ponies in the mornings. Make sure you come back in an hour or so and we'll go and fetch your saddle."

Tom skipped down through the main yard. It was bustling with activity as lads went from stable to stable, mucking out horses, sweeping down paths and walkways and getting ready to ride out their first horse, saddles and bridles slung over arms.

Down at the ponies' yard, Sarah was just about to start mucking out Leo. "I'll do that," said Tom as Leo nickered his greeting.

"That's very kind of you. I'd love to get those Butler kids out first thing for mucking out, but all they are interesting in is riding, and that's not very often."

"I love it all," said Tom rubbing Leo's forehead and kissing his muzzle.

He quickly cleaned out the stable and then helped Sarah sweep down the yard. She left grooming Leo to him while she got on with the other ponies. Undoing Leo's rugs, he brushed him all over, flicking off the dust and picking the bits of straw from his mane and tail. Leo loved being groomed. His skin quivered and his bottom lip drooped and every so often he sighed with satisfaction. Tom felt his front legs, wondering if they were normal temperature or not, and then replaced his rugs.

After about an hour he said to the pony: "I'll be back in a bit Leo. I forgot your saddle so we need to go back home and fetch it."

When he appeared in the kitchen, Dixie thrust a piece of warm buttered toast into his hand and grabbed her car keys. She ushered him into her car and they followed the narrow lanes back to Hilltop House. Before long they arrived at the top of the driveway. Tom glanced towards the sand school and, aghast, screamed at Dixie to stop the car. She did so in a flash. Tom flung open the car door and went racing across the sand school to where Hannah was riding Skip. In her hand she had a thin schooling whip. She thrashed it down over and over again across Skip's hindquarters screaming: "You will jump you stupid pony."

Skip was drenched in sweat and shaking with fear. He took a few steps forward but stopped in front of the jump and again the blows rained down on him. He trembled, his ears back, saliva coming from his mouth as she jabbed the bit and kicked and hit him at the same time. Hannah didn't notice Tom approaching until he tried to drag her off Skip yelling, "Get off that pony. Get off him. Get off him."

"Get away runt," Hannah screeched. "This pony will jump." And she kept beating him.

Tom put himself between Skip and the whip and Hannah hit him across his arm. He flinched and a sharp pain seared through him. By this time Dixie had reached them: "Get off that pony now," she shouted at Hannah.

Hannah looked panic-stricken. She had had no idea Dixie was there. The wife of the country's top trainer had seen her hitting the pony. This would end her hopes of riding in races. She knew she couldn't explain her behaviour and the racing world was a very small community. People would soon hear about how she lost her temper with Skip. Nevertheless, she jumped off the pony and started making lame excuses. "It was his fault. He wouldn't jump and it's dangerous for Emily."

"Emily hates jumping," said Tom furiously. "And so does Skip. There's a reason he won't go over jumps. Maybe he had an accident one day. You should never have hit him to make him jump."

Dixie was fuming and grabbed the reins from Hannah. "I do not want to hear another word from you. That was the most appalling display of horsemanship I have ever seen."

Still struggling to contain herself, Hannah blurted out, "The pony deserved that, for humiliating me by not jumping," then she strode towards her car and drove off with a screech of tyres.

Tom held his arm, which was throbbing in pain.

"Are you OK love? Can you manage for a bit longer while we sort Skip out?" Dixie asked.

Tom nodded, biting his lips together and trying hard not to cry. If one blow on his arm hurt this much, Skip must be in agony he thought. Dixie soothed Skip until he stopped trembling. He had huge welts across his hindquarters that were oozing with blood.

"Tom, love, I'm going to call the vet. Just to be on the safe side. Then I am going to ask Sarah to come over and see to the ponies and Chilli and Elvis this evening and tomorrow until everyone else comes back."

"Do you think you should call the Heavens?" he asked.

"Yes definitely, but we'll do that in a little while. They can't do anything from London. We'll make sure Skip is comfortable and see what the vet says first," she said.

She led Skip away. He could barely walk he was so sore and gingerly made his way back to his stable where the horses whinnied to him reassuringly. Half an hour later, another car skidded down the drive and the vet jumped out.

"Thank goodness you're here," said Dixie. "This poor pony has been beaten with a whip. The girl riding him was in a frenzy and was beating him over and over and over again."

"Who's the girl?" mumbled the vet as he grabbed his kit from the back of his car.

"Hannah Oatway."

The vet nodded. "That doesn't surprise me. I've seen her lose her rag before." He came from the other side of Todbury and he explained that one of his clients owned a livery yard where Hannah had worked the previous summer.

"I don't think she'll be trying to find a job around here again," said Dixie.

Skip stood in the stable with his head hanging low. His sides were still heaving and his coat felt clammy.

"He's in shock and pain, but he'll be fine. I'll treat him now, and clean up where the whip has broken the skin. He'll need to be checked every hour or so."

Dixie pulled her phone from her pocket and called Sarah. "Sweetheart, could you come over to the Heavens' please and keep an eye on one of their ponies. He's been badly beaten."

"No problem at all. I've finished the ponies here," Sarah said, without asking any questions.

"I'll look after the ponies at Hall Farm," offered Tom.

Dixie shook her head. "I don't think so. You can hardly move your arm. Let's take a look now."

She helped Tom take off his jacket and pull his jumper over his head. His upper arm was red, tender and swollen, and Tom winced as Dixie gently prodded it. "That's going to be a little sore, but its just bruising. You'll get a rainbow of colours over the next few days," she said.

Tom looked very glum.

Reading his thoughts, Dixie added: "If you rest it today, you should just about be able to manage the racing rally tomorrow."

He nodded his head eagerly.

After the vet had left, Dixie bustled around the yard. "It doesn't look like Hannah has even mucked out here," she said, going from stable to stable.

Tom helped as much as he could, carrying sections of hay

and straightening up rugs. Every so often they checked Skip, who had perked up a lot.

"Time to call the Heavens and tell them the news," Dixie said finally, sitting on an old chair in the tackroom. Tom sat beside her on the wooden trunk where they kept the horses' rugs. "But before I do, there's a question I have to ask you." Tom nodded, wondering what was coming. "The saddle. Mandy was absolutely convinced she had packed it, and was really sorry that it meant a trip here today to fetch it. You took it out of the Land Rover didn't you?"

Tom gulped, thinking he was in serious trouble. Dixie quickly said, "Oh, no, don't worry. I should have said you are not in trouble at all. If it wasn't for you, goodness knows what would have happened to Skip. I'm just curious about what made you do it."

"I didn't like Hannah," he said.

"What did she do to upset you?"

"Nothing. I can't explain it," he felt unable to describe the uneasy feeling he had when he first met her.

"Well thank goodness you didn't. You're obviously a very good judge of character."

Sarah arrived wearing a pink waterproof coat that was far too big for her and a pink woolly hat with a bobble. She put a huge bag in the tackroom, and then went from stable to stable, handing out carrots before talking to Dixie and Tom. She was so full of energy and warmth, the whole yard lit up in an instant.

"Bit of bad news here then?" she questioned. "The ponies are all fine at home, by the way, and Leo seems quite settled. I think he feels quite important. He can see the racehorses as they go up the gallop, so I've told him he'll be going up it himself tomorrow, and I'm sure he nodded," she laughed.

Dixie gave Sarah a spontaneous hug.

"So what happened here then?" Sarah asked.

"Poor Skip has had a terrible ordeal at the hands of a freelance groom called Hannah. She was helping out while the Heavens are away, and is supposed to be riding for them too during the winter."

"Was she loud, with long brown hair, scraped off her face in a pony tail?" Sarah asked. Tom and Dixie nodded at the same time. "It's not the first time she's been caught being rough on a pony," she said.

"Sarah, what on earth are you carrying in that bag?" asked Dixie, changing the subject. She didn't want Tom to hear any gossip that he might repeat.

"Just a few bits and pieces to keep me going. I'll stay here for another couple of hours, just to make sure Skip's OK."

"You're a star Sarah, thank you so much," said Dixie. "Come on then Tom, time we went back to Hall Farm."

Tom stood up to go and winced as his arm started to throb again.

"Before you go Tom, let me just rub some special cream on your arm. It's marvellous stuff."

"You and your lotions and potions," laughed Dixie.

Chapter 16

The next morning Tom sat in the old leather sofa in the Butler's kitchen glued to the television watching replays of races. Whatever Sarah had put on his arm, it was already feeling much better. He was mesmerised by the speed with which West Is Best jumped the hurdles in one of the races, and didn't notice the Heavens peering through the window. He didn't hear them open the door and he didn't realise they were all watching him until Emily could contain herself no longer and blurted out: "I'm sorry Tom."

He jumped, and then saw the whole family smiling at him. 'Well this is all a bit confusing,' he thought, 'Why are they staring at me?'

"Um hello," he ventured. "Did you have a nice time in London? I thought you were coming home this evening."

Mrs Heaven sunk into the sofa next to him and, putting her arm around him, said, "After what happened with Skip we decided to get up early and drive straight back home. We cannot thank you enough for what you did yesterday."

"We've got a little surprise," Emily interrupted. "Well a few actually," she said thrusting a large plastic carrier bag onto his lap.

He delved in and pulled out a navy silk shirt with white stars on it and buttons down the front. There was also a navy silk skullcap cover dotted with stars. Then he pulled out a pair of white racing breeches, and a pair of leather racing boots. They were exactly like the clothes he'd seen the jockeys on the telly wearing, and he opened his mouth in amazement. "Are these all for me?"

"All for you," said Emily. "As a thank you. 'Cos none of us believed you about Hannah. And we should have listened. And I'm sorry too."

"What are you sorry for?" he looked confused.

"I'm just sorry, you know, for being a bit tricky."

"She means she's sorry for getting jealous," piped up Ted.

"Can't say I'd noticed," shrugged Tom.

"How's your arm?" asked Mr Heaven.

"It feels a lot better than it did yesterday. Sarah put some well weird stuff on it that stank. I think I'll be able to ride Leo later on today."

"We had a great time in London, but we really missed you," said Emily.

"Did you? Why?" asked Tom. He was so used to feeling invisible, it seemed strange to him that anyone should miss him.

"We all missed you Tom!" said Mr Heaven smiling.

"Oh," Tom said not really taking in their outpouring of affection, he was so busy wondering when he would be able to try on his new racing kit.

Suddenly Mr Heaven held his hand out to Tom.

"What's that for?"

"Grab it and you'll see."

Tom took hold and Mr Heaven pulled him to his feet. Tom stood in front of him, looking confused.

"Feel anything?" asked Mr Heaven.

"Er, nope," he said.

"Fit as a fiddle. Come on let's go and get Leo ready for the racing rally."

Tom's eyes lit up, as he realised what Mr Heaven had done.

"You're right. My arm doesn't hurt at all!" he said, shaking it just to be sure.

Down at the ponies' yard, Leo stamped his foot impatiently, whickering furiously as soon as he saw Tom. Tacking him up quickly, Tom led him out of the stable. Leo could sense excitement in the air. He carried his head high and his ears were pricked forward as far as they could go. He jigged as if he was on tiptoe and snatched at the bit. His coat gleamed in the autumn sunshine and he snorted at the other ponies who all peered over their stable doors. Leo knew everyone was looking at him, and he grew taller and prouder, loving his moment in the limelight.

"He's a born show off that one," laughed Mr Butler appearing around the corner with Ben. "Are you ready Tom? You certainly look the part, but there's just one thing missing." He had something behind his back and now revealed it with a flourish – a racing saddle. "I hear you've been riding with your irons short already, so I think you'll be fine with my old pony race exercise saddle," he continued, expertly swapping the saddles over.

Tom grinned from ear to ear.

Ben disappeared to get Mr Happy while Mr Butler legged Tom up onto Leo who grew more excited by the second.

"Keep him walking. Just canter to the halfway point up the gallops a couple of times so that we don't wear out Leo too much before the rally starts," advised Mr Butler.

Tom rode the pony over to the large sandy area where he'd seen riders walk their horses before heading out of the yard. He sat very lightly on Leo's back, his stirrups up short, keeping soft and relaxed. Leo started to calm down and by the time Ben arrived on Mr Happy he was walking happily on a long rein.

Mr Butler called to Ben and Tom. "Walk down to Halfpenny Lodge and then trot back up to the gallops. We'll grab the Gator so we can watch everything from the viewing platform."

"Okay guv'nor," said Ben.

Leo strode out beside Mr Happy matching his strides. Mr Happy looked over at the little pony and gently nuzzled his neck, as if he was telling him not to worry about a thing. Ben chatted away to Tom, telling him about the races he'd recently won and the horses he'd ridden.

"Who's your favourite?" asked Tom.

"I can't really say that I have a favourite as they are all very special in different ways. But I have a huge soft spot for Francome. He's a very special horse. He's so fast over a fence. When you're a jockey you ride a lot of mediocre horses, and you have a fair few falls, but it's all worth it when you sit on a horse like Francome."

At Halfpenny Lodge they turned their horses to trot back up the hill. Tom watched Ben and copied the way he stood in his stirrups, taking the weight off his horse's back. They soon came to the entrance to the gallops. They could see the Heavens and Butlers up on the viewing platform, their binoculars trained on them.

"OK Tom, we'll go upsides twice, very, very slowly. I'll talk you through everything, but first things first. Do you know how to bridge your reins?"

"Yep," said Tom. "I bridge my reins when Leo's feeling bouncy. If I keep my hands really still, he always relaxes."

"And it's the same up the gallops. If you move your hands on the reins, you'll give Leo something to fight against. Whereas if you keep them very still, and rest them either side of his withers, he'll relax," said Ben.

Tom nodded, taking in every word.

Ben leant down and adjusted Tom's foot in the stirrup. "You can either push your foot right through the stirrup so that the metal bar is clamped against the heel of your boot. Or you can balance on the ball of your foot. Whichever is most comfortable."

Tom moved his foot from one position to the other, and then opted for the ball.

"Ah, I see you prefer looking up with the times than adopting the old pasty foot," laughed Ben.

Tom had no idea what he meant.

Ben continued, "When we set off, push your weight into

stirrups and keep your lower legs in tight to the saddle."

This sounded quite confusing to Tom, so he nodded eagerly and decided to do what came naturally to him.

"OK we'll set off very slowly now, so bridge your reins and off we go."

Tom set off on Leo, close beside Ben on Mr Happy. He kept very still in the saddle. Ben glanced over and smiled.

"Flatten your back by bringing your nose closer to Leo's neck. We'll just keep at this very steady canter. No need to do much more. It will build Leo's fitness too."

They approached the viewing platform where Emily waved eagerly. Tom's grin widened. Ben pulled up before the gallop veered to the right towards the schooling ground.

"That's far enough for the first time, bearing in mind Leo's a pony and he's got an hour or two at the rally later. We'll walk back down and next time up we'll quicken the pace and see how you feel about that."

They set off again and, as the pace quickened, Tom felt a burst of elation. The wind rushed against his face. Leo stretched his neck as he reached forward with his legs. Tom crouched down low against his neck. "Come on," he urged. Leo's pink nostrils flared. Tom felt as if his heart was beating in time with Leo's pace.

Ben quickened again on Mr Happy. "Keep him as close as you can, to give him a sense of being in a race," he called.

Tom nodded. It amazed him that Ben's voice sounded crystal clear. Standing on the side of the gallop all you could hear was the thundering of hooves. Yet on horseback, you could speak to the person beside you. They flew up the gallop, the horses' loud breaths in harmony with their pounding hooves.

"We'll pull up at the top of the hill. Just say 'whoa', stand up a bit and Leo will slow to a trot."

Tom did as instructed and in a smooth transition, Leo slowed to a trot and then came back to a walk.

"How do you feel Tom?" asked Ben.

"Brilliant. That was just brilliant." Tom's cheeks were pink and his eyes watering. He felt slightly out of breath too. Leo snatched the bit in anticipation. "Steady boy," said Tom.

"You're breathing nearly as hard as Leo," laughed Ben. "I think you'll need to do some running around your fields to get fit as well."

Tom puffed away. "Why do you need to be fit when you're just sitting still on the pony's back?" he gasped.

"It's the speed you're going and the fact it's harder to fill your lungs with oxygen," said Ben.

Tom nodded, promising himself he wouldn't let his pony down by not being fit enough.

The Butlers and Heavens had assembled at the bottom of the viewing platform.

"Boy's a natural," roared Mr Butler. "First time up the gallop and he sits like an old pro."

Tom pulled up in front of them his face alive with excitement. "That was amazing and Leo was so good," he said.

"You were pretty good too Tom," said Mrs Heaven smiling.

"Tom you need to trot steadily back up the gallops, go out onto the lane and beyond the woods, where you'll see the schooling rings. There's about two acres of all-weather surface up there," said Mr Butler.

"Is that where the rally is?" asked Tom.

"Yes, you'll find a dozen or so kids there with Mickey who'll be teaching you, along with Ben here."

"I'll be up in a minute Tom, after I've seen to Mr Happy," called Ben.

"We'll come up too Tom," called Mrs Heaven.

Tom suddenly felt shy. He wasn't sure how he felt riding with strangers. He hesitated. Leo sensed his indecision and grabbed at his bit.

Mrs Heaven walked over to him. She gently placed a hand

on his knee and said: "Don't worry Tom. Ride like nobody's watching and concentrate on Leo and everything you've been taught at home."

Tom gulped and then shook his head. "I can't do it," he mumbled.

"Of course you can Tom. You'll be fine. And anyway, no one will be looking at you. They'll be too busy riding their own ponies."

"But what if I make a fool of myself and then Leo looks silly?"

"You won't Tom. You're one of the most natural riders any of us has ever seen. Go on. Don't think about it and just ride!"

"But what will we have to do?"

"I should think you'll be in a group of half a dozen and you'll be taught things like how to ride with short stirrups and how to bridge your reins."

"But I already know all that," said Tom.

"So you'll be fine then, won't you?" said Mrs Heaven.

Tom was nearly convinced. "Come on Leo," he said, "Let's do it," and they set off up the gallop to the corner of the field and slipped through the gap in the hedge. Tom patted Leo on the neck. "Just you and me now," he murmured as he walked through the gate.

Horse lorries, and trailers were parked up in rows. Children scurried around giving their ponies a final brush off before jumping on board. Parents barked orders.

Leo took in all the sights and sounds.

It all seemed chaotic until, as if summoned by a silent cue, one by one the children mounted their ponies and filed towards the gate that led into a vast all-weather school. It was 1pm, the start time for the rally.

Mr and Mrs Heaven arrived with Emily, Ted and Ben. Tom was relieved to see them. Ben dashed off to the middle of the school, leaving the rest to huddle around Tom.

"Come on Tom. Let's go and meet the DC Mrs Pemrose."

Tom had no idea what a DC was but followed Mrs Heaven towards a lady holding a clipboard at the entrance to the school.

"Ah Tom, how very pleased I am to meet you," the woman trilled, ticking his name off on her list. "I am your District Commissioner, or DC," she continued. "There are two groups today, eight in each, and you're with Ben Steed over there. He's a top jockey you know. One of the best in the country."

Tom nodded and glanced over to where Ben was talking to a row of seven children. He breathed a sigh of relief. 'Maybe these rallies aren't so bad,' he thought to himself. He took his place at the end of the line of riders, and stood next to a small girl with long brown hair tied in a ponytail. She was on a pretty chestnut pony that had a dished face and carried his tail out at an angle.

Tom looked at her shyly. "Hello," he said.

"Hi," she replied, seeming just as shy.

"What's your name?" asked Tom.

"I'm Verity and this is Malteser. I'm nine."

"I'm Tom, this is Leo and I'm nine too."

Once the ice was broken, they chatted away while Ben walked down the line of ponies and inspected all the tack, checking it was safe.

"OK kids, I'm Ben Steed and I'm a professional jockey, but I started off in the Pony Club and did exactly what you are doing now. I went to plenty of rallies, rode in a lot of pony races, took a few Pony Club tests, and here I am teaching you lot all about it!"

They all grinned, nodding furiously at the same time. Ben was quite a name in the Pony Club world. Not only had he won a lot of pony races, but when he was much younger he had also ridden show ponies and once won the supreme championship at the Royal International Horse Show. The girls all adored him. Some even had pictures of him pinned to their walls.

"First things first. How to bridge your reins," Ben said demonstrating with a spare set he'd brought with him.

Tom felt more at home by the minute.

"Next we're going to put up your stirrups a few holes."

They all hitched their stirrups up and practised walking around. Verity stayed by Tom's side.

"This feels a bit uncomfortable," she said.

"Drop them down a hole and you'll be fine," said Tom, jumping off Leo so that he could hold both ponies. Verity sorted her stirrups out and Tom leapt back on.

"Now with your feet you can do a full pasty, balance on the ball of your foot, or just the tip. Whatever feels most comfortable because there are no hard and fast rules," said Ben.

The children giggled. "What's a full pasty?" asked Verity.

"It's when you wedge your foot in right to the heel. It keeps you feeing secure, although some people find it difficult to get their balance. Stand up in your stirrups and see what feels best."

They stood up and shifted their feet about until they felt comfortable.

"OK let's try trotting. Bridge your reins, rest them over your pony's withers and try just standing in your stirrups," shouted Ben.

After a couple of minutes he called them back into a line. "Next we're going to canter, seat out of the saddle, hands steady on the wither. Tom you lead off."

Tom felt in his element as Leo steadily cantered around.

Satisfied that the ponies weren't about to go bolting off into the distance, Ben said they were ready to come up the gallops to the halfway point. Tom oozed with confidence and led the way to the bottom where Mr Butler gave them more instructions. One by one they set off back up the gallop, going steadily and getting used to riding with their stirrups short and keeping their hands steady. Tom kept the pace very steady and could hear the sounds of the ponies' hooves behind him. Leo made it feel very easy as he covered the ground towards the top of the hill.

Tom slowed right down and Verity caught up with him on Malteser.

She grinned. "This is just brilliant," she said sitting neatly on her pony.

"Are you going to be at the pony races?" asked Tom shyly as they trotted then slowed to a walk.

"I think so. At least I'd really like to. Do you think I'll be good enough? You look really professional and I've never really done this sort of thing before."

"Of course you'll be good enough. You were brilliant and Malteser loved it too. Didn't you boy?" said Tom reaching over and patting the little chestnut's neck. "I only started riding in the summer, so it's all new to me too," he added reassuringly.

"But you look so amazing," said Verity in surprise. They chatted away together as they watched the rest of the ponies already walking and huffing and puffing as they made their way up the gallop.

Ben was waiting for them at the top and he laughed. "I think you'll need to get your ponies a little fitter if you want to have a go at pony racing." The children assembled around him, and he gave them a few last words of advice: "Just remember you haven't won until you've crossed the line, so you need to keep your head down, keep riding, and do as much as you can to win."

While the other children went back up to the schooling rings to find their parents, Tom trotted down the hill, his hands on the buckle end of the reins. He felt like singing, he was so happy, and hummed away to himself until he was back at the yard.

"Cake anyone?" called Mr Butler jumping out of the Gator beside Tom and the Heavens a few minutes later. "Have some tea and cake and then you can all head back to Hilltop House. Not that I am trying to get rid of you of course. You know me. Spectacular way with words."

Tom fussed around Leo, washing the sweat away carefully and feeling his legs like he'd seen Mr Butler do.

Mickey peered over the door. "Well. I see you did good there."

Tom looked up. "Huh?"

"I see you did good there. Up the gallops. Just now."

Tom blushed. He wasn't used to all this praise.

"That pony'll be grand now. You go in and get your cake."

"I'll just check his legs again."

"It's no good checking his legs until he's cooled right down this evening."

"Oh, is that why it's done at evening stables?"

"Quite right," said Mickey. "So he'll be grand just there. Come on. I've been invited in to the big house too. Good job too. I love Mrs Butler's chocolate cake."

They walked up the yard together, Tom trying hard not to skip, he felt so happy.

Chapter 17

Tom sat on the floor rubbing his saddle furiously. Emily perched next to him, covered in water as she rigorously cleaned her reins. Ted was on the chair with his stirrups leathers over his knees, rubbing saddle soap into them.

Tom's bridle was in bits beside him. "What's the point in having a tack inspection when it will only get dirty again?" he said, wondering how he was going to reassemble it.

"You have to be spotless for the rally, ready for the inspection when you get there," said Emily.

"Then what do you do?" asked Tom.

"Oh fun stuff like trotting in circles, practising changing the rein, cantering, and stuff."

"Sounds really boring to me," said Tom.

"It is but the jumping's really good fun," said Ted.

Tom's eyes lit up.

"Do you get to jump those coloured jumps like in the school?" he asked.

"Just like that. Although, of course, Skip and I will leave that bit out," said Emily.

Early the next day they set off together, their tack gleaming and their ponies shining. The ponies' hooves clipped clopped along the lane that led to Mrs Irving's where the Pony Club rally was being held.

As they walked through the gateway to the field, a prim lady wearing long brown leather boots, jeans, a tweed jacket and a hat that looked to Tom like it might once have been living, hurried over to them waving a clipboard.

"Emily, lovely to see you. You're in Yellow Group over there with Hannah. And you've brought your new little friend Tom," she said nodding in Tom's direction. "Pleased to meet you, Tom. I am Mrs Irving, but most of the children know me as Mole. Not sure why," she continued as she pushed her glasses up her nose which was sharp and pointed and reminded Tom of a carrot, except it wasn't orange.

'I wonder if that's why they call her Mole,' he thought to himself as she twitched it rapidly. She thrust a hand out to Tom who obligingly shook it and then said: "You're in the same group as Emily. And Ted, so lovely to see you, too. You're in Green Group with Sammi."

"Um, who did you say we were with?" ventured Tom.

"Hannah," replied Mrs Irving moving off to greet the next arrivals.

Tom whispered to Emily: "Did you hear that?"

"Yes I did. They can't have heard about her. What are we going to do?"

Tom thought fast. "Well, they won't believe us if we tell them. We're just two kids, no one will take any notice. We need to somehow let people see what she's really like. We need Skip not to jump so that she loses her temper."

Emily quivered. "No. No way. Not if she's going to hit Skip."

"We'll stop her before she does that. But we need her to get really cross. She'll start yelling and then everyone will see."

Ted said: "As soon as she starts ranting I'll get everyone in my group to watch her, too."

"But it's not fair on Skip," wailed Emily.

"Well what do you suggest then? She's still teaching, and she's probably still hurting ponies," said Tom crossly.

Emily thought hard, but she couldn't come up with any other ideas.

"OK, we'll do it," she said, "but she's not to scare Skip."

They lined up in Hannah's group with four other children.

Hannah inspected all the tack making comments as she did so. Under their riding hats and in their best riding clothes, she didn't recognise Tom and Emily, and she barely noticed the ponies because she was so intent on criticising the children's efforts at tack cleaning.

A few minutes later she started their lesson. She asked them to walk around on each rein for a few minutes, moaning about their poor positions in the saddle. Next she asked them to trot on a circle while she put up a tiny course of three show jumps. She instructed them to jump and one by one the ponies cleared the poles until it was Skip's turn. He skidded to a halt.

"Bring him around again and kick," shouted Hannah.

Emily did as she was told, and Skip stopped again.

"Do it again and kick," yelled Hannah, her voice getting louder.

Ted looked over from his group and brought Henry to a halt.

"That pony will jump. Hit him," screeched Hannah again.

One by one all the children stopped and stood staring at Hannah, as she grew more and more angry. Emily brought Skip around again. By now he was trembling.

"It's OK Skip, I won't let anything hurt you," she said as she pretended to kick him.

Hannah stormed over. "Get off that pony now and I am going to ride him and make him jump."

"You mean like you did when you beat him up?" Tom said loudly.

"Shut up," said Hannah fiercely.

"No," retorted Tom and said again, more loudly this time: "You mean you want to beat him up again?"

Emily marched over on Skip. "We all know what you did to my pony."

"Shut up. You have no idea what you are talking about," said Hannah. She was getting angrier by the minute.

"You beat him up. Look here's a scar on his hindquarters."

"Liar," shrieked Hannah and, completely beside herself, she went to lash out at Emily with her riding whip.

"Oh no you don't," said Mrs Heaven who had just arrived in the Land Rover. She grabbed the stick before Hannah struck Emily. "You've been caught red-handed. You should not be allowed anywhere near animals or children."

Hannah stood shame-faced. Everyone had witnessed her about to hit Skip. "You need to sort yourself out Hannah, and learn to manage your anger before you get yourself into very serious trouble," continued Mrs Heaven. "And for your information, there is a reason Skip doesn't jump. He is scared because he was injured badly in a fall. One day he may find his courage again, but until then, we are not going to force him to jump."

Mrs Irving joined them. "I am afraid Hannah you will have to leave. We cannot tolerate this behaviour. You are supposed to be setting an example to the children, and not the type of example that involves hurting animals."

Hannah looked like she was about to explode. She opened her mouth to say something and then thought better of it. She scuttled off to her car, and left the field in a cloud of exhaust smoke.

Mrs Heaven took the remainder of the lesson. It flew by with Mrs Heaven calling out instructions and Tom enjoying every single second. By the end, he was jumping small fences and Skip was happily trotting over poles on the ground. Tom forgot all about the other children watching him when it was his turn. He was completely focused on Leo and, in fact, when he knew they were going well together, he even quite liked the idea of having an audience.

'It's not so bad after all,' he thought to himself. 'All I need to do is concentrate on riding and on Leo, and it doesn't matter who's watching.'

As they rode back to Hilltop Farm, Tom, Ted and Emily talked about how they had caught Hannah.

“And I can’t wait until the pony race now, and I don’t mind who watches me. I reckon I wouldn’t even mind if it was the Queen” said Tom with relief.

Emily shrieked: “I’ll be your number one fan at the pony races.”

Ted grunted. He was never sure what all the fuss was about.

Chapter 18

Tom hardly ate a thing all week. Every time he went to eat, his stomach felt like it had a million butterflies flying around in it.

"Why aren't you eating Tom? You're so skinny, it's not like you have to lose weight to ride in the race," said Emily at tea time.

"Emily, leave Tom alone. He's nervous about the race tomorrow. Aren't you Tom?" asked Mrs Heaven.

He nodded. But he wasn't nervous. He was petrified. It was all he could think about and he couldn't sleep. It wasn't that he was scared. He couldn't wait to ride in the race. It was that he was worried he'd let everyone down, especially Leo. He'd made a list with Mrs Heaven so that he knew what to expect.

- Arrive at the pony races.
- Take Leo out of the box.
- Go and get changed.
- Weigh out.

And at that point, thinking about the list, he'd panic, wondering how he could be warming Leo up and changing at the same time. The problem was he had no idea of how a race day worked. No matter how many times Mrs Heaven reassured him that everyone would be there to support him.

"All you need to think about is how you ride Leo," Mrs Heaven had said, several times.

He'd thought about that a lot too and decided that as Leo had a good turn of speed, he'd hold him back and then kick him on when he could see the winning post. He had considered going flat out from the start, but Leo would never keep galloping for that long. And anyway, Ben had come up with the same tactics, reassuring him that when the other ponies were tiring, Leo would pick up speed.

Tom's race was the '138cm and under Novice Pony Club Members' Only Race', the last race of seven on the Pony Club race day. The distance was seven furlongs, or just under a mile, and there were ten ponies taking part.

The evening before the race, Tom checked and re-checked his kit bag: silks, body protector, crash helmet, boots, breeches, racing saddle and whip. He'd need all those things to weigh out. He mulled over the race again, remembering everything Ben had taught him. Even so, he tossed and turned in his sleep all night, imagining he was riding in a race and there were ponies thundering all around him.

He woke up early and bleary eyed, and then, with a jolt, remembered that the pony race day had finally arrived. His tummy felt so tight he couldn't eat any breakfast.

"Come on love. How about a bit of toast?" asked Mrs Heaven. "You won't last all day if you don't eat."

"I'll eat later, I promise," said Tom.

They packed up the Land Rover and then got Leo ready. He had smart navy blue travel boots and a rug to match. Tom paced the yard until at last Mrs Heaven called, "OK let's load Leo."

He led the pony towards the trailer, but when they reached the ramp, Leo stood at the bottom refusing to walk in.

"Come on Leo," said Tom and pulled the rope. Leo pulled against him. "Oh I remember. If I pull, you'll pull too," Tom said slackening the rope.

"Tom just stay very relaxed," called Mrs Heaven. "He'll walk in a minute. He's just a bit wound up as he can sense the excitement. He's probably been watching you walking around the yard!"

Tom took a deep breath and sat down on the bottom of the ramp. Leo walked up to him. "Come on then boy, follow me in," said Tom and he scrambled to his feet as Leo obliged.

As they set off, Leo whinnied shrilly as if he was wondering where he was going and fretting about leaving his friends. Tom barely said a word all the way there. Mr Heaven and the other children sang daft songs to keep his mind off the races.

'There once was a boy, whose name was Tom,
And his pony was called Lee-oh.
They went to the races to run in a race,
And they won, they won, they won-oh.'

"Is that the best you can do, Dad?" laughed Ted.

"Yep," said Mr Heaven. "Why don't you all join in?"

Soon they saw the signs for the field where the races were being held. They were directed to the lorry park where they parked beside a huge lorry, which must have had room for a dozen ponies. Tom looked at it wide-eyed, thinking it seemed very professional.

"Don't worry about the lorry," said Mr Heaven watching him. "It's a client of mine. He runs a horse transport business and, trust me, there's one very small pony in there, ridden by his daughter. His other lorries are all on the road that's why he's using that monster!"

"Come on then Tom. Let's go on the course walk," said Mrs Heaven.

There were several children assembled outside a tent. 'Weighing Room and Secretary' was written in bold black letters on a white board beside it.

"That's where we'll declare Leo when we get back," said Mrs Heaven, "and that's where you get ready," she said pointing to another tent that said 'Changing Room'.

There were other children waiting for the course walk and excitement filled the air as they talked about their ponies. It seemed to Tom that he was the only one who was nervous. They set off with a man who introduced himself as Colin Burd. He was quite small and said he'd once been a flat-race jockey. "Now I ride in point-to-points. Much better as I can more or less eat what I like," he laughed.

They made their way to the far side of the field where there were two white markers. "This is where you'll start. You'll come down here, your girths will all be checked, and then you wait for the starter to call you in. No jumping the gun, so to speak."

He set off along the course and the children followed him eagerly.

"It's measured in furlongs. Anyone know how many are in a mile?" he asked.

"Eight," yelled all the children, except Tom, who knew the answer but was too shy to shout.

"That's right. You've been doing your homework. Your races are either seven or eight furlongs. So, those racing at seven furlongs will start here," Colin said pacing forward for several strides.

Tom took in every single word and started to imagine he was actually on Leo.

"There's quite a bend here, so take a pull and make sure you have control of your ponies. Otherwise you'll be wanting to veer right, and your ponies will keep going in a straight line and end up in that pond over there," Colin pointed. "You've got these white plastic rails here to help guide you."

Tom eyed up the winning post in the distance, gauging in his mind how long it would take to get there. He decided he would start to kick on as he approached a huge oak tree where the track straightened out for the last two furlongs.

"And this is where you'll be wanting to see how much petrol your ponies have got left in their engines," said Colin at more or less the same time.

Tom felt a huge wave of relief. 'Maybe I know a tiny bit about what I am supposed to be doing,' he thought.

"Keep aware of what all the other ponies around you are doing, but keep riding to the line. The race isn't won until you've crossed it, and all too often I've seen jockeys stop riding over those last crucial few yards," Colin advised.

He asked the young jockeys if they had any questions.

"If we're right at the very back and our ponies are too slow, should we just trot back?" asked one child.

"Well you can if you like, but I'd keep cantering if I were you. It's all good experience."

By the time they reached the winning post, quite a crowd had appeared. They milled around with their dogs and children.

"Come on Tom. Let's go and check on Leo, then, when it's time for your race to weigh out, we'll be ready to grab your kit, and declare," said Mrs Heaven.

They walked back to the lorry park where Emily was fussing over Leo, Mr Heaven was reading a veterinary journal in the front of the Land Rover, and Ted was furiously tapping away on his tablet. Leo nickered when he saw Tom, and stamped the floor of the trailer in anticipation. His eyes were huge and bright with expectation behind his thick lashes as he watched the comings and goings of the field. Every now and again he tossed his head. Tom put his hand on the pony's nose and he shoved it away, snorting as he did so. His muscles were taut and he looked like a pent up ball of energy, ready to gallop.

Tom grinned. "You're ready for this aren't you boy?" he said.

The first of the races was underway and Tom watched intently. These were the more experienced children who sat stylishly on their ponies, their stirrups up short. Their brightly coloured silks flashed by as they thundered towards the finish, the crowd cheering them on. The commentator called the race, growing more and more excited as the winning post approached, and Leo stamped his feet, eager to be out of the trailer and galloping like the other ponies.

After the third race, Mrs Heaven took Tom over to the changing room to get ready. Then he stood on the scales with his saddle and the clerk checked his weight.

"You wait quietly now in the changing room until you're called, and I'll go and tack up Leo. Don't worry about anything. It's all supposed to be fun," said Mrs Heaven.

Tom sat very quietly waiting until it was his turn to ride. He felt amazing in his new kit – 'Just like how a jockey must feel,' he thought.

Some of the other children joked with each other, but Tom preferred to keep himself to himself. He wanted to focus on the task ahead of him. He could hear the crowd's hurrahs and hand clapping every time a race finished. 'One more to go and then it's me,' he thought, and went over his race plan again in his head.

At last the children were called into the paddock where Leo shimmied around, taking quick light steps while Emily tried hard to keep hold of him.

"Ted, go and grab the other rein before Emily lets go. Leo is quite wound up by the whole thing," said Mrs Heaven.

She walked with her husband to the centre of the paddock, ready to leg Tom up. "Do you think Tom's going to be OK? We hadn't reckoned on Leo being quite this alight."

"We'll soon find out," said Mr Heaven as Tom approached.

"OK Tom?" he asked, just as Ben also appeared and thrust a pair of goggles into the boy's hand. "No self-respecting jockey can ride without a pair of goggles," he said.

Tom was so pleased to see Ben he was lost for words. "Isn't that the jockey Ben Steed?" he heard one of the other children ask her parents. He felt so proud to be standing in the paddock with one of the best jockeys in the country. He just hoped he didn't mess everything up.

Finally, ten ponies were in the paddock, gleaming and shining in the early winter sunshine. Their number cloths with the white figures stood out boldly against their blue backgrounds. The ponies were full of anticipation for the race ahead but they walked steadily, except Leo who had huge springs in his steps. The bell rang. Emily and Ted led Leo into the centre. They could barely keep hold of him he was so lit up with excitement.

"Tom, just be sure to sit light, bridge your reins, and go with Leo if he gets a bit jumpy," advised Ben. He legged Tom up and the boy sat softly in the saddle. "I'll take him now kids," Ben said, holding the lead rope softly and rubbing Leo's neck.

Leo threw his head up, just missing Tom's nose. "Now you're a fizzy boy," said Tom unperturbed by Leo's bouncing. He just kept stroking the pony's neck quietly talking to him.

"That's exactly right, Tom. Sit quietly. Don't tense up. Go with him."

They walked another two circuits of the paddock and Leo started to calm down a little, just as the steward at the exit directed them on to the course. Three ponies were already cantering steadily away.

"Good luck," said Ben as he slipped the lead rein and let Leo go.

As soon as Leo started cantering, he settled into a steady rhythm. It was as if he knew the job he had to do. They cantered to the start where the other ponies were circling. Tom joined them and Leo walked calmly around, standing still while his girth was being checked.

"Um, who's going to make it?" asked Tom.

"Do you mean who is going to go first?" asked a boy wearing bright yellow silks.

"Yes. Because I'm going to go steady on my pony," replied Tom.

"Me," shouted a girl with a long brown plait down the centre of her back wearing purple and navy silks and sitting on a pretty chestnut pony. It was Verity from the Pony Club rally.

"Oh hi Verity. Good luck," called Tom.

"And good luck to you too," she replied. "We're parked next to you in that huge lorry as dad's other ones are all working today."

"Verity, no chatting, you need to concentrate now or you'll miss the start," Tom warned.

"Come on in then," shouted the starter. "No flyers. Just walk very calmly and slowly to the line."

The children obediently did as they were told and the ponies jigged to the line.

"OK, on you go," the starter called, bringing down his flag.

A girl in pink silks kicked her pony on and set off at a fierce pace. Leo jumped off and pulled at the reins. Tom held onto him, and kept him close to the rail, tracking the two ponies in front of him. Out wide was the boy wearing yellow silks, and behind came three other ponies. Apart from the girl in pink, who was several lengths ahead, they were all closely grouped and kept at a steady pace.

At about the halfway marker, Tom pushed Leo on and he picked up speed, grabbing the bit. Tom brought Leo wide to join the two ponies in front and the three raced side by side. The winning post was in sight. Tom saw that the pony in front was starting to tire. Leo kept galloping. He began to pull away from the other ponies. One length, two lengths, three lengths. 'Keep riding,' thought Tom. 'Don't stop until you've crossed the line.' Leo flattened his back and reached forward with his legs. Tom pushed his shoulders further down and started moving his arms in rhythm with the pony's strides.

"Come on Leo," he urged.

Leo kept giving more. Tom glanced to his left and saw the boy with yellow silks gaining ground. He pushed Leo on again, getting even lower in the saddle. Leo's nostrils flared, his ears were back, and he gave one last effort, stretching and reaching. They were over the line, Leo's muzzle just inches in front.

Tom pushed on for a bit longer, just to be sure, and heard the commentator call: "First, Leo, second, Dazzling Dynamite and third, Malteser."

He stood in his stirrups and punched the air as they cantered on down the course. "We've won Leo!" he shouted and then felt relieved he hadn't messed up. He lent down and hugged the pony.

"Steady boy," he said, standing up in his stirrups again and bringing Leo back to a trot.

Emily, Ted, Ben, and Mr and Mrs Heaven rushed across the course. "Well done Tom. You've won!"

Tom blinked back the tears.

Ben winked: "Don't you go crying now."

They walked towards the paddock as the commentator announced again that they had won, and walked over to the number one spot. Tom leapt off, undid the girths and slipped his saddle off. A photographer took some photographs, and Tom left the paddock to weigh in but not before he gave Leo another huge hug. "Thank you Leo, for saving me," he whispered.

Mr and Mrs Heaven, Emily and Ted all hugged him as he made his way to the weighing room, while Ben led Leo back to the trailer.

Tom stood on the scales and pinched his arm hard. He couldn't quite believe he had won. But then he heard the announcer call the official result over the loud speakers and he finally knew he really had won his first ever pony race. He also knew it was the best thing that had ever happened to him, apart from meeting the Heavens. He changed quickly and rushed back to the trailer. As they crowded around him, he became lost for words. Mrs Heaven raised her finger to her lips and, as silence fell, Tom said, "Th-th-thank you for everything," and then added, "I think we should tell my mum. It might cheer her up."

Mr and Mrs Heavens nodded. He didn't have to say any more.